KIOWA RISING

When the stagecoach to El Paso is ambushed by robbers, the only passenger able to take a lead in resisting the bandits is retired provost marshal Talbot Rogers. Not only must he lead the other passengers to safety, but he also finds himself carrying word to an army base about an imminent Kiowa uprising. With a band of outlaws dogging his steps and a young woman to protect, it will be a race against time for Rogers to warn the outpost at Fort Williams of the danger about to engulf it.

Books by Jack Tregarth
in the Linford Western Library:

CHISHOLM TRAIL SHOWDOWN

JACK TREGARTH

KIOWA RISING

Complete and Unabridged

LINFORD
Leicester

First published in Great Britain in 2017 by
Robert Hale
an imprint of The Crowood Press
Wiltshire

First Linford Edition
published 2019
by arrangement with
The Crowood Press
Wiltshire

A catalogue record for this book is available
from the British Library.

ISBN 978–1–4448–4308–8

Published by
F. A. Thorpe (Publishing)
Anstey, Leicestershire

Set by Words & Graphics Ltd.
Anstey, Leicestershire
Printed and bound in Great Britain by
T. J. International Ltd., Padstow, Cornwall

This book is printed on acid-free paper

1

On a fine summer's evening in 1859, a bright red Concorde stagecoach was bowling briskly along a dusty track in northern Texas. The Butterfield mail coach was heading south-east, towards El Paso, although there was little chance of reaching that town for a few days yet.

The unofficial motto of the Butterfield company was 'Always room for one more' and judging by the three men perched precariously on the roof of the stage, this worthy, commercial principle was being sedulously adhered to. Inside the coach, eight more passengers were sitting so closely packed that their knees were dovetailed together. These men and women were a mixed crew. Tucked in one corner, squashed almost breathless by a generously built lady of mature years, was a colourless and insignificant-looking little man of perhaps five-and-forty years of age. He had boarded only a few hours earlier and promptly fallen asleep. Now he had awoken and, as the stage rattled its way along through the barren landscape, this man eyed up his fellow passengers and did his best to read their characters.

Seated opposite the man in the corner was a young fellow of lusty and virile appearance. He was, by the look of him, about twenty-five years old and sported not one but two pistols, which bounced up and down on his thighs every time the coach went over a bump. Sheer ostentation, thought the little man to himself. One pistol is plenty and enough, always providing you know how to use it. He dismissed the young man facing him as being most likely a show-off and braggart. Bully and coward too, I shouldn't wonder, he thought shrewdly.

Next to the youngster was a married couple, solid and respectable types. Farmers, perhaps.

The man occupying the corner seat next to the window, diagonally across from him, was a harder study. This individual was probably about the same age as he himself, which was to say forty-six. Most noticeable was the peg-leg which stuck out awkwardly across the floor of the compartment.

As he was sizing up the strange figure, the other man looked up sharply and caught his eye. For a fraction of a second, their eyes met. In that instant, Talbot Rogers decided that the two of them were of the same 'breed. The other man seemingly came to a similar conclusion, because his lips twitched slightly and he gave an almost imperceptible nod in Talbot's direction. Then he turned away and gazed out of the window.

Having satisfied his curiosity about the three men and one woman on the opposite seat, Talbot Rogers was about to repeat the exercise with those sharing his own side of the coach. Before he was able to do so, there came a sharp but distant crack, which he guessed to have come from the rocky hills which lined the track along which they were careening.

'Rifle,' he said instinctively. 'Maybe half a mile over there to the left.'

The words were scarcely out of Talbot's mouth, when the coach juddered and slowed. Then came the hollow boom of a scattergun right above their heads. The man with the wooden leg said in a conversational tone of voice, 'That'll be the messenger riding shotgun, up yonder. Though what he hopes to accomplish with a scattergun at that range is a mystery to me.'

Talbot had been thinking precisely the same thing and he realized that he had been right about the man with the false leg; they were indeed two of a kind. The fat woman sitting next to him exclaimed, 'Lord a mercy, what are we to do?'

'Nothing much to do, ma'am, other than to wait on circumstances,' said Talbot reassuringly.

'Is it Indians, d'you think, or what?' she asked anxiously.

'Bushwhackers, more likely,' ventured the man with the wooden leg. 'I'll hazard a guess and say as they've shot one of

4

the horses, so's to slow us down a mite.'

There came a second rifle shot and again the stage shuddered, beginning to slow down even more. Talbot Rogers said, 'That'll be another of our horses done for. Best to do now would be for the driver to rein in, and him and his partner to throw down their weapons.' No sooner were the words out of his mouth, than he heard the driver shout something and then there was a scraping of iron as the brake was applied.

There wasn't, to Talbot's mind, the apprehension of any great danger. Like as not, a half dozen men would come riding up directly and relieve them of all their cash money and any jewellery that the ladies might have on display. He noted the seed-pearl ear bobs on the farmer's wife sitting opposite and wondered if she would have the wit to remove them and place them in her bag. The woman at his side was dripping with various rings, necklaces and bracelets, but they were so many and varied that Talbot guessed that they were all of them probably no more than Pinchbeck and paste.

There is no action so foolish or wicked that somebody, somewhere will not undertake it, and although Talbot Rogers had already gauged that this current affair would most likely end with little more than a slight inconvenience to the travellers in the mail-coach, he could not have predicted that one of the men riding atop of the stage would take it into his head to make a fight of it. It was against all reason, but there it was. Just as the stage was grinding to a complete halt, some of the men clinging to the roof commenced firing.

Sitting next to the driver was a hot-headed young man who had only recently been discharged from the army. When the first shot was fired at the coach, killing one of the horses drawing it, his instinctive reaction had been to raise his own weapon and return fire. At a range in excess of 800 yards though, he might as well have used a pea shooter as the sawn-off scattergun with which he actually let fly. His action, although making not the slightest difference to the man with the rifle who was crouched up in the rocks overlooking the road, set a very bad example to two of the passengers riding the roof. No sooner had the driver's companion loosed off a shot in the general direction of the hills, than they drew their own pieces and began scanning the horizon for targets.

Soon after the first of the horses had been shot, another rifle shot came from the hills and at the same moment, those on the outside of the coach saw four riders emerge from a gully and begin cantering towards them. Whereupon the most incautious of the men on the roof snapped off a couple of shots towards the approaching men, guessing quite correctly that they were bandits, intent upon robbing the stage.

All that the inside passengers knew of the affair was a sudden cacophony of pistol shots from overhead and away to one side. Automatically, they all began huddling down, away from the windows, lest a stray ball should come flying through. As it happened all the fire from the attackers was directed at the men on the roof and in the driver's seat.

The coach swayed and veered off the road. As it did so, there was a resounding, splintering crack from beneath, which Talbot took to be one of the axles breaking on a rock. By the time that they came to a halt, the driver and guard were dead and so was one of the men who had been riding on the roof. Of the remaining two, one had taken a flesh wound and the other, who had not even taken out his own gun, was quite unscathed.

The woman next to Talbot Rogers said breathlessly, 'Heavens, what's to do now? Are we all to be murdered?'

'I wouldn't say so, ma'am,' replied Talbot quietly. 'You must expect to be robbed, but other than that, I don't see any harm befalling us.' They could see from the window that four riders had now reined in by the coach. All had neckerchiefs pulled up over their mouths and noses and gave the impression that they were not men to be trifled with. The man with the false leg said in a low voice, 'Don't any of you folk play the fool now. These boys'll be good and mad and it won't do to provoke 'em.'

Truth to tell, none of the men and women in the compartment looked in the least as though they were looking for a confrontation. Apart from Talbot and the fellow with the peg-leg, they all appeared terrified out of their wits by the turn of events. Talbot Rogers noted with quiet satisfaction that he had been spot on in his estimation of the young man's character. The poor young fellow was pale and trembling with fear. Just as I suspected, thought Talbot to himself, coward, as well as a braggart.

From outside came a harsh command for them to come out with their hands held high. 'If we see so much as a twitch from anybody, as looks like a move towards a gun, then 'fore God, we'll kill every mother's son o' you!' the speaker promised.

There was little to be done, other than to open the doors and climb down as slowly and cautiously as could be.

Nobody had the least doubt that the man who had issued the warning, meant just precisely what he had said.

Up on the dusty rocks overlooking the road, Ramon Mercador sat at his ease. Not yet thirty, Mercador was a veteran of various obscure wars in Central and South America. He was renowned for his prowess with a rifle and was invariably allotted the task of bringing down the horses in enterprises of this sort. Hitting a moving horse at half a mile was something that Mercador could do in his sleep. Having halted the coach, he now saw no urgency in making his way down to join his comrades in their task. The brief gun battle was over and it looked as though things were now well in hand. Pulling out his tobacco pouch, Ramon Mercador rolled himself a cigarette and settled down for a leisurely smoke.

★   ★   ★

Even after the death of the three men who had been riding the outside of the stage, the robbery could have passed off peacefully with no further bloodshed, if only one of the bandits had been able to focus his mind entirely on that end, without being distracted by other longings. When they stepped out of the stagecoach, the riders invited all the men to throw down their guns, which were then gathered into a little heap. Talbot, who looked about as menacing as a clerk in a grocery store, was not carrying a pistol at his hip. The men who were robbing them had dismounted and one announced that his friend would be coming round with a leather saddle-bag and that the women should cast into this every piece of jewellery that they were wearing or had concealed about their persons. The men were similarly told to put all their money in the bag.

'And let me catch any one o' you holdin' back so much as a cent and I'll

11

kill that man with my own hands,' said the leader of the band.

Now that they were all out in the open, Talbot was able to look over the people who had been sharing his bench during the journey. His heart sank when he saw that in addition to the fat woman who had been sitting next to him, there was a man travelling with a young girl whom Talbot took to be his daughter. She was little more than a child; so young that she had not yet begun to put up her hair. She could have been no more than fifteen or sixteen at the most. By the look of her, this girl was young and innocent enough to find the experience of being robbed in this way a novel and exciting one, for she gazed around with shining eyes, perhaps thinking how she would turn the adventure into a story to tell her school friends.

While one of the bandits went from passenger to passenger with his bag, collecting money and valuables, one of the other men noticed the girl and went over to her.

'Well, ain't you the pretty one?' he said and raised his hand to touch her cheek. Her father moved forward and before anybody knew what was happening, was knocked brutally to the ground by the man who was showing such interest in his daughter. The others from the coach watched helplessly, not knowing how matters might develop.

As for Talbot, he knew very well what would most likely happen next. These villains would hoist the girl over one of the saddles, ride off with her and use her as they saw fit.

The man who was evidently the leader of the outfit came wandering over and said to the one who was pestering the girl, 'What's this? Somethin' to share around?' The odd thing was that when he later thought about the scene, all that Talbot was able to recollect about this fellow was that he had around his neck a garish scarf or neckerchief, which was bright yellow in colour.

For answer, the other man moved behind the girl and then clamped his

13

hands around her; one on each breast. She gave a shriek of horror and her father made as though to leap to his feet. The third member of the gang, who had noticed that something interesting was happening, came up at that moment and lashed out with his foot, sending the girl's father sprawling back in the dust. Of all the crimes that he had encountered in his long career, none ever filled Talbot Rogers with more loathing and contempt than the rape of women. He viewed it as the lowest and most unmanly action possible.

Imperceptibly, Talbot Rogers moved a little closer to the group clustered around the young girl. As he did so, he glanced across to the other passengers, none of whom seemed minded to do anything helpful. He caught the eye of the man with the false leg and directed his gaze meaningfully to the heap of pistols which the robbers had confiscated from their victims. The man gave the merest nod, which Talbot took to mean that he would be ready when the action began. Why he felt that of all the men who had been on the coach that this was the only one who would be any use in a straight fight, Talbot could not have said. But he was in the habit of trusting his instincts and they had never yet played him false.

There could be no doubt now that three of the men who had waylaid the stagecoach had rape, as well as rapine, on their minds. The one who was collecting money and jewellery kept looking over to the others, presumably anxious that he wasn't left out of the fun. The girl herself looked as though she was on the point of fainting. The one who had first molested her was running his hands over her body from behind, while his two comrades looked on, laughing and making coarse jokes about letting the badger loose.

Casually, Talbot Rogers stuck his hands in his pockets and took one more step sideways, until he was only four or five feet from the man holding the helpless girl. All the pieces were now in place and there was no point in delaying matters further. In one fluid movement, Talbot withdrew his right hand from the pocket of his jacket and stretched out his arm, pressing the little Derringer into the ear of the man who was grasping the frightened girl's arms. Then he pulled the trigger.

Out of the corner of his eye, Talbot was pleased to observe that the man with the wooden leg was already diving towards the pile of weapons which had been taken from the passengers. For a man with such an impediment, he surely moved fast. The man Talbot had shot fell sideways at once, like a felled tree, a gout of blood spurting from his ear. Without hesitating for the least fraction of a second, Talbot turned and shot the nearest of the other bandits, sending the .44 bullet straight through the man's right eye. Just before he fired this second shot, he was aware of shooting starting away to his right and assumed that the fellow with the peg-leg was in action.

Having used both barrels of the little

muff-pistol, Talbot Rogers was now unarmed and could only hope that his enemies were in a similar condition. He whirled around, expecting at any moment to hear the crash of gunfire and to feel perhaps the sickening impact of a ball striking him in the chest, but there was dead silence. Even so, he dived down at the pile of pistols, snatched one up at random, cocking it with his thumb as he did so, and then turned warily to see if any targets presented themselves.

Four or five men lay prone on the ground and it took Talbot a few seconds to figure out the play. All the bandits seemed to be dead and he scanned those standing, looking for the fellow with the false leg. Then he saw him, lying on his back a dozen feet or so from Talbot. Talbot stood up and went over to him, but he could see at once that nothing could be done. There was a small hole in the front of the man's shirt and judging from the position of it, he must have taken a ball right through one of his lungs. From Talbot's experience, he guessed that blood loss would kill the fellow in no more than ten or fifteen minutes.

Squatting down at the wounded man's head, Talbot said quietly, 'Well, I reckon you must have settled with two of them. Leastways, I know I accounted for two and I don't see any of 'em alive now.'

'Yes, I got them both, but one of them got off a shot, too. It was bad luck.'

'You'll be all right. We'll get you patched up.'

The man shook his head impatiently and said, 'There's no time for a heap of foolishness like that. I'm dying. You need to help me.'

'Surely,' said Talbot, 'you want a drink or aught?'

'No, I mean you got to do something for me. Reach into my pocket, there. Inside my jacket.'

As Talbot's hand brushed against the man's ribs, the fellow winced in agony. From the pocket, he extracted a long white envelope, addressed in exquisite

18

copper-plate to Officer Commanding, Fort Williams.

'This what you mean?' asked Talbot.

'Yes. Listen carefully now, for we don't have much time.'

2

'My name's Carson and I work for the Indian Bureau,' said the dying man. 'Three days back, I received intelligence that the Kiowa are about to rise. Word is, the Comanche'll run with them.' The effort of talking had seemingly exhausted Carson, for beads of sweat were glistening on his brow.

'Take it easy,' advised Talbot. 'Surely this can wait?'

'I had you pegged for a man of sense. You know full well, that I'm not long for this world. Just listen, don't talk.' Talbot Rogers shrugged and said nothing.

'Night o' the full moon, that's four days hence, there's going to be a raid on Fort Williams. You know it?'

'I went there once,' said Talbot. 'Cavalry base, with a little town next to it. It's as peaceful as can be up there, from all I'm able to apprehend.'

'Gates are wide open. People go in and out, trading and such. Indians too,' said Carson.

The other passengers from the coach were standing around, looking like they didn't know what to do next. The girl that Talbot had rescued was tending to her pa, the rest were talking in low voices. None of them came over to interrupt the conversation between Talbot Rogers and the man whose life could surely be measured in minutes now. They all seemed to understand that the two men speaking together had found some kind of common bond; although what that might be, none of them was able to guess.

For some reason, Talbot felt the urge to make an uncharacteristically fatuous remark. He said, 'You were in that much of a hurry to get to Fort Williams, I wonder you rode the Butterfield and didn't just take horse.'

'Ever tried riding a horse when you've only one sound leg?' asked Carson irritably.

'Can't say as I have,' admitted the other man.

'Then stop asking a lot of damn fool questions and attend to what I say. The Kiowa are after the arsenal at Fort Williams. The place isn't in posture of war, it's open to all. Once that falls, all the territories right down to the Mexican border will be at the mercy of the Kiowa and their friends. There's even a rumour as the Apaches might be in on the game. They got scores of their own to settle.'

'What would you have me do?' asked Talbot quietly, keenly aware that the man lying in front of him was nearly dead. As Carson was speaking, little red bubbles were appearing around the wound in his chest. Like a child's soap bubbles, they grew a little and then burst, proof positive that the ball had taken him through the lung.

'That's the fellow,' said Carson appreciatively. 'Here's the game. You take one o' those horses right now. Leave these folks to shift for their own selves and make haste to Fort Williams. Hand over that letter and give 'em chapter and verse of how you came to receive it from me.'

'That's all? Just carry on the way I was headed anyways and deliver this letter?'

The wounded man had closed his eyes, as though he were suddenly weary. Talbot wondered if he had slipped into unconsciousness, but a second later Carson opened his eyes and fixed him with a piercing gaze, saying, 'Mind you do as I've said, now.' His eyes flickered shut again.

Wholly at a loss to know what to say, Talbot ventured, 'You want I should say a prayer or something?' There was no answer and as he watched, Carson took a deep breath, gulped and then breathed out again slowly. He didn't draw breath again.

Tucking the letter which the dead man had entrusted to him into his pocket, Talbot Rogers stood up and looked about him. Eight people, seven standing and one lying on the ground, stared back at him. He had the impression that they were now looking to him for counsel and advice on what next to do. Having seen him and Carson deal so sharply with the four men who had attacked the stage, they presumably expected him to pull a rabbit out of the hat now and transport them all safely to the next town. First things first, thought Talbot and went around where the luggage was stowed and began pulling at the tarp which protected the trunks and bags from the dust.

* * *

Having rolled his cigarette, Ramon Mercador leaned back against a smooth and comfortable boulder and closed his eyes, inhaling the fragrant Virginia tobacco contentedly. He calculated that by the time he had finished his smoke, his friends would have completed their depredations down below and he could saddle up and join them as they made their way back to the town where they had been staying.

The sudden and furious outbreak of shooting down below took Mercador quite by surprise. He opened his eyes in amazement and peered down to the barren plain through which the road wove its way. His first guess was that one of the passengers might have offered resistance and been shot down by two or three of the members of the gang as a reward for his impudence. Gazing now at the figures gathered around the stage-coach, which at this distance had the appearance of a child's toy soldiers, Mercador saw at once that he had been grossly mistaken. He could see that one of the victims of the shooting was Bill Hilton; even at half a mile, the yellow neckerchief which covered the lower half of Hilton's face was quite distinctive.

'What the hell . . . ?' muttered Mercador and sat up sharply to see what he could make of it all. Truth to tell, he knew that the robbery must have gone terribly wrong, because although Bill Hilton lay there, perhaps stone dead, nobody seemed to be firing at the passengers in order to avenge his death. Which meant that, incredible though it was to consider, all four of his companions had been killed or otherwise incapacitated in the brief flurry of shots which he had heard. Snarling an oath, the swarthy bandit leapt to his feet and unhitched his horse from the bristlecone pine to which he had secured her. Then he began picking his way carefully down the narrow trail towards the scene of the ambush.

* * *

From a battered carpet bag, Talbot Rogers extracted a pistol with an exceedingly long barrel. This he tucked into his belt. Then he took out a box containing brass cartridges and reloaded his little Derringer. The others watched the drab and colourless little man, wondering what he would do next. In fact, he looked up sharply and said in an urgent and commanding voice, 'You people get behind the stage here!' He gestured in the direction which he wished them to go. Then he said, 'You men take pistols from that pile. Don't bother whether it's your own, just arm yourselves.'

The lone rider which Talbot had spotted was at the foot of the low range of hills now and was surely heading in their direction. It might be nothing to do with the case, but he was mindful that that was the self-same direction from which had come the rifle fire that had killed two of their horses. Once he had shepherded everybody out of the line of fire of the fast approaching horseman, Talbot knelt down and withdrew the strange pistol from his belt. He cocked it carefully and then leaned the barrel on the rear wheel of the coach and sighted down it, drawing down on the rider.

As Mercador came to the level ground at the foot of the hill, he saw that all the people, men and women both, who had been standing round near the stage, were now scurrying to get behind it. He was no coward and perhaps the best shot in Texas into the bargain, but mounting a frontal assault on a defended position in this way would be madness. He supposed, quite correctly, that the male passengers would by now be armed and mightily ticked off with him and his compadres. They'd open fire before he was a hundred yards from the stage; of that he had no doubt at all. Regretfully, he reined in and then spurred on his horse, back the way he had come. The sooner he reached Tom Hilton and told him of the death of his brother, the better.

The young man whom Talbot had dismissed on first sight as a cowardly braggart, confirmed this view of himself by shouting, 'Hooee, that's one of 'em who couldn't face a fair fight!'

'He'll be back with his friends 'fore long, or I'm a Dutchman,' said Talbot, ignoring the youngster. 'We best get clear of here and the sooner the better.'

'What do you propose, sir?' asked the man who had been sitting opposite Talbot on the coach, the man he had figured for a farmer. 'Can we get this vehicle moving, do you suppose?'

Bending down and surveying the state of the front axle, Talbot shook his head. 'It's pretty well mashed up,' he said, 'we've neither the time nor tools to remedy it. It'll be shanks' pony or horse riding for us, I guess.'

'We've four horses with saddles and four without,' remarked the farmer thoughtfully, 'and nine of us. The sums ain't lookin' too bad.'

'What about you ladies?' asked Talbot. 'There's no question of riding side-saddle or any such nonsense. Are you all three able to ride a horse, straddling it like a man?'

The farmer's wife blushed to hear such plain speaking, but the fat woman who had been squashing Talbot during the journey laughed and said, 'Needs must when the Devil drives. I can manage.' She turned to the young girl and said, 'What about you, honey?'

'I've grown up with horses,' said the girl shyly, 'I can manage well enough, I think.'

'That's the spirit, miss,' said Talbot, giving her a broad smile. 'I have to say, you're bearing up remarkably well after all that's happened. How's your pa?'

The man who had been travelling with the girl was sitting on the ground, nursing his jaw. He looked to Talbot to be in pretty poor shape. Looking round at this group of ordinary people thrown into an unexpected and frightening situation, Talbot Rogers felt a surge of compassion. He knew that before he breathed his last, the man called Carson had expected him to mount up and abandon these folks, for the greater good. If Fort Williams were to be destroyed and the troops there killed, then there would be nobody to protect the straggling line of settlements which stretched out into New Mexico. Eventually, of course, the government in Washington would send an army to restore order, but by that time, hundreds, perhaps even thousands of farmers and settlers might have been massacred.

Despite the unassailable logic, which required that Talbot Rogers should leave these eight men and women to fend for themselves, while he went haring off to warn the army at Fort Williams what was afoot, he knew that he would never be able to face himself if he left the passengers from the stage to live or die as they were able. They were a pretty sorry crew, from what he could see, and he knew that they would fall prey to the first bunch of Indian warriors or bushwhackers who might chance upon them. Sure, he would carry Carson's letter to the commander of the fort, but he would first have to take these folk to safety.

★   ★   ★

When the Hiltons and their gang had fetched up in the town of Indian Creek, the citizens of the place had at first

31

sensed a business opportunity. Their town was off the beaten track and not many travellers came through. The arrival of a band of fourteen men had looked like the chance to raise prices and skin the passing travellers for as much as could be squeezed out of them. After all, tough as they looked, these men would be wanting rooms to stay in, whiskey to drink, horses shod and provisions to take with them when they left.

They say that man proposes, but God disposes and in the present case, the Lord evidently had other ideas about how things were going to work out for those living in and around Indian Creek. If there was any exploiting to be done or advantageous bargains to be struck, then the Hilton brothers and their men figured that it would be they who would be dictating the terms. Although the farmers and storekeepers in the area were fond enough of carrying pistols at their hips, they were unaccustomed to using them and any shooting which did take place was generally against wild animals or Indians. Even that was by no means a common occurrence and the guns which the townsfolk carried were really little more than badges of masculine pride.

With Tom and Bill Hilton, the case was very different. They carried guns and were all too ready to use them at the drop of the proverbial hat. One circumstance which had a slight bearing upon subsequent events was that both the Hilton brothers were dandies in their own way. They habitually used clothes brushes to remove dust and dirt from their apparel, and both men also affected brightly coloured silk bandanas, tucked around their necks. Tom's was red and his brother's yellow. These, they regularly washed, so that the colours showed clearly.

On the night that the fourteen riders hit town, they found their way without delay to one of the two taverns in Indian Creek. For the first hour or two, things went well enough, with all the members of the gang throwing money around freely. As the evening wore on though, many of the usual patrons of the Silver Dollar began to drift off and move across the road to the Lucky Lady, the rival drinking establishment. They had begun to get a feel for the kind of people that the Hiltons and their boys were and did not wish to be around when the tough-looking crew became completely intoxicated. It wasn't until nearly all the usual customers had left that the two Hilton brothers noticed anything amiss and when they finally realized that although it was still light outside, the saloon had almost emptied; they took it to be an insult.

'What is it with the people in this damn town?' Tom Hilton asked the barkeep truculently. 'You're an unfriendly bunch of cows' sons, you know that?'

The man behind the bar shrugged and kept his own counsel. He was perfectly capable of maintaining order in the bar when it was only a matter of one or two drunks to turf out and he had even been known to respond in a lively fashion when a cowboy began shooting up the place; he was not, however, up to handling fourteen heavily armed men.

'You'll have a drink with us, won't you?' enquired Tom Hilton of the bar-keep, an unmistakable note of menace in his voice. Since the fellows who had driven away all his other regulars were spending freely and looked to be a more profitable bunch than the dirt farmers who usually drank in his place, the man behind the polished, wooden counter smiled cheerfully and accepted the offer of a whiskey.

At this point Jack Martin, the owner of the Silver Dollar, felt that by taking a drink with these men, he had defused the situation and smoothed things over neatly enough. That was until Tom Hilton caught sight of a man sidling off towards the bat-wing doors, clearly doing his best to be inconspicuous about it.

'Hey, you!' called Hilton, 'Where are you headed?'

'Time I was off to feed m' hogs,'

replied the man, reasonably enough. 'I only came in for one drink an' I've been here longer'n I ought.'

For some reason, the man's answer seemed to infuriate Tom Hilton and he said, in a voice choked with anger, 'Hogs, is it? That your idea of a joke?'

The man standing a dozen feet from the door looked perplexed at the notion that he had made any sort of a joke, saying, 'No, sir, that ain't no joke. I got thirty hogs I'm raisin' an' if'n I don't get home to give 'em their vittles, they're apt to go hungry.'

'Well then,' said Hilton, 'where's everybody else skedaddled off to? Answer me that, if you can. Strikes me as folk in this here town are an unfriendly crew and that's a fact.'

The hog-farmer scratched his head in bewilderment, hardly knowing what to say, when Tom Hilton detached himself from the bar and walked over to the door, blocking the man's way out. He said, 'I had enough o' you people and your ways. Looks to me like none of you want to be in the same room as us boys.' Members of the gang exchanged meaningful glances. They were used to Tom's sudden and irrational bursts of anger, especially when he was drinking. None of them felt inclined to get involved in the business. The only one who could handle Tom Hilton when he was in this mood was his brother Bill and he didn't give the appearance of a man who was going to intervene.

The farmer stood watching Hilton, by no means sure what the play was. He was, as he had intimated to the other, truly just concerned with getting home to feed his hogs. On the other hand, he was a proud man and he didn't see why he should allow anybody to push him around in his own town. Some of this man's feelings must have shown on his face, for Tom Hilton said, 'I'm telling you now, fella, you want to leave this bar, you're gonna crawl out on your hands and knees.'

'The hell I am!' muttered the farmer and moved forward a little until only twelve feet or so separated him from the bully who was blocking his way out of the saloon.

'What was that, you son of a whore?' asked Tom Hilton, cupping his hand to his ear as though he were a little deaf. 'You say what?'

Hearing such a deadly insult, touching as it did upon his mother, the hog-farmer said in a low voice, 'You best get clear o' that door now.'

'Make me.'

This was just the sort of pointless and violent confrontation in which Hilton gloried. Those who rode with him had seen a number of similar scenes played out in bar rooms, cathouses and corrals across three states. All those standing at the bar of the Silver Dollar watched breathlessly to see what would chance next.

The farmer was carrying and was not in the least a coward. He hadn't always raised hogs for a living and in fact, had served as a scout for some years on the frontier. Although he realized that the man facing him had, for purposes at which he could only guess, manoeuvred him into fighting in this way, the farmer was not about to back down. He went for the pistol which he habitually wore when in town. He had almost cleared the holster when the first of Tom Hilton's bullets took him in the chest. The second followed a fraction of a second later, passing straight through the man's forehead. He was dead before he even hit the ground.

When the echoes from the roar of gunfire had subsided, Hilton turned to those in the saloon and said, 'You all saw him draw first. I ain't answerable for his death.'

From a strictly legalistic viewpoint, this was perfectly correct, but it did not alter the fact that those in the Silver Dollar that evening had seen cold-blooded murder committed and there wasn't a thing any of them were either willing or able to do about it.

There was not a lawman within thirty miles of Indian Creek and even if there had been one nearer at hand, it is doubtful in the extreme if he would have taken any action against Tom Hilton. After all, what had been witnessed by two dozen men? Two fellows had bandied a few words with each other and then one of them had gone for his gun with the evident aim of killing the other. The man who had been in danger of death had then proved quicker than the other and shot down the aggressor. It was as clear-cut a case of self defence as you could hope to see.

The killing of Joe Sutton, for that was the name of the unfortunate fellow who had been so needlessly gunned down, set the tone for the rest of the Hilton brothers' stay in Indian Creek. Having shown that they would kill a man for no better reason than that he was on his way home to feed some hogs, others in town began to take good care not to annoy either the Hiltons or the men who were riding with them. If eyebrows were raised by one of the Hilton gang about the cost of some provisions they were buying, then the storekeeper hastily lowered the price. When they took their horses to the smithy and remarked that they didn't look to be chiselled out of too much for the farrier's work, then the bill was adjusted until it barely covered the cost of the materials used; never mind the labour involved.

This was how the Hilton gang lived from day to day. They preyed on anybody weaker than themselves and by killing somebody the very day that they rode into town, they ensured that the other citizens of Indian Creek got the message good and early. Supplying goods and services at a loss to this bunch of cutthroats struck most of the folk in town as a pretty good bargain when the alternative was being shot down in some trifling dispute about leaving the saloon early.

The Hilton gang had been in town for less than a week when one of the men revealed that he had heard some interesting intelligence about the Butterfield mail coach which was due to pass twenty miles south of the town the next day. The rumour he'd picked up was that there might be a bunch of bearer bonds in the mail sack being carried to El Paso. These were as good as cash and it was worth hitting the stage, just on the off chance that there was some truth in the story. If nothing else, they would be sure to pick up some jewellery and cash from the passengers and so Bill Hilton, Ramon Mercador and three others set off to see what they might get on such an enterprise.

3

Talbot Rogers was not a man to put himself forward, but he could plainly see that unless he took a hand, the surviving passengers from the stage would just wander around like headless chickens until they died of thirst or were massacred by hostile Indians. It was a nuisance, but he would not feel easy until he had guided them all to safety. The fact that there were three ladies in the case clinched the matter for him. He would never rest easy again in his bed if he just rode off and left them to their fate.

Despite deciding that he should aid them, Talbot's diffidence caused him to say tentatively and apologetically to the group at large, 'I don't rightly know what you all plan to do next. For my own part, I have business in Fort Williams and so I'd be happy to accompany any of you who are heading in that same direction.'

Talbot's offer was met with such an immediate response, that he knew at once that he had been right and that all the others had been looking to him for a lead and half expecting him to rescue them from their present predicament. One matter demanded his attention before they set off and that concerned the young man he had been sitting opposite during the journey. He was satisfied in his own mind that he had been right about the youngster and that he had displayed cowardice when danger threatened. Since the shooting had ended though, Talbot had, to his disgust, noticed the young man winking and smiling at the young girl who had come so very near to being raped. It looked to him as though the fellow was flirting with the girl, and one who could scarcely be more than sixteen. That, thought Talbot to himself, was something which he would need to nip in the bud without further delay. Before discussing any plans for their progress to Fort Williams, Talbot approached the young man and asked if he would favour him with a few words in private.

Having drawn the boy out of earshot of the others, Talbot said in a friendly voice, 'You saw how I served the last fellow as troubled that young lady, I suppose?'

At first the young man did not seem to catch Talbot's drift. When he did, he stuttered a denial. 'Hey, I didn't mean nothin' by all that. I's only joshing with her, tryin' to keep up her spirits and such.'

Talbot Rogers said nothing more, but simply looked searchingly into the man's face, until he felt that he had got his message across. During this scrutiny, the boy flushed and began to look uncomfortable. At length, he said, 'Yeah, all right. I get the idea. I'll steer clear of her.'

Talbot patted him on the arm in a fatherly way, saying, 'That's right. I knew we wouldn't fall out about it.'

Before setting off, Talbot suggested that they introduce themselves to the others. He began by telling them that he was a travelling salesman and that he was on his way to Fort Williams. The young man was called Tim Hogan and didn't seem to be travelling anywhere in particular. 'Just movin' along' was how he put it. The middle-aged man and his daughter, who was fifteen, were on their way to El Paso, where the man was to take up some clerical job with the customs service. His name was Clarence and his daughter was Melanie. After the fat, cheerful woman had introduced herself as a singer of some kind, the couple whom Talbot had assumed to be farmers confirmed him in that view. They were on their way to visit relatives near Fort Williams. The two men who had been travelling atop of the stage gave no clear information about themselves and Talbot guessed that they were escaping some trouble or other.

'Question is,' said Talbot, 'how we're

going to travel. There's four horses tacked up and ready to go and we can take two of the others from the stage, use them to carry our water and such like.'

'What of our bags?' said Mrs Littlechild, the farmer's wife.

'We travel light,' said Talbot. 'It may happen that you see your luggage again, but I wouldn't lay odds on it.'

The woman seemed disposed to argue the point, but Talbot thought they'd delayed long enough for introductions and other such niceties. He said firmly, 'Ma'am, you mistake me. I'm not telling you that you must leave your bags behind. Nothing of the sort. I'm only setting out how those as want to throw in with me will be arranging matters. If you and your husband, or any of you others for that matter, wish to strike out alone, why, you go right ahead.'

Her husband said in a low voice, 'Hush up now, Marianne. This gentleman's offered to guide us, we must go by his rules.' Marianne Littlechild bridled a little, but said nothing more. Nobody else objected to abandoning their belongings in that way and without further ado, Talbot directed the order in which they would be travelling.

The girl Melanie was set on one of the horses and Belle, the singer, had another. It seemed only right that the man who had been wounded in the gun battle should also ride, although Talbot Rogers's private opinion was that he wasn't that badly hurt. From all he could see, there was no more to the case than a scratch to his thigh.

Mrs Littlechild flatly refused to straddle a horse and announced that she would sooner walk on her own two feet. Since there were no saddles for the other mounts, Talbot got Tim Hogan to lend a hand and they cut loose the traces of the horses which had been pulling the stage. Then they loaded these two and the other spare mount up with water kegs, the little food that was being carried and also the rifles and other weapons which had been carried by the driver and his companion. Talbot detached the tarp which had been covering the boxes and trunks and rolled that up too and slung it over one of the horses, figuring that they might be able to rig up some kind of shelter for the ladies.

Before they began, Talbot asked if anybody had any maps or knew where the next settlement along the way might be. It appeared that nobody did and so the six men, three women and half dozen horses set off south-west in the general direction of Fort Williams and El Paso. Young Melanie and the older woman who had mounted up cut a ridiculous and faintly indecent spectacle with their petticoats all rucked up and almost displaying their drawers. One was too young to be bothered about the impropriety of their position and as for the older, Talbot had a shrewd notion that she might be in the habit of revealing considerably more than just her underthings to the world.

★　★　★

A mile from Indian Creek, Mercador reined in his horse and thought carefully about what he was going to say to Tom Hilton about the death of his beloved brother. They might have been as rough as all get out, but nobody who knew the Hiltons ever doubted for a moment that they thought the world of each other. It might have been different if it had been Tom who was dead and Ramon Mercador was bringing the news to Bill. Bill had been a mite slower to take umbrage than his brother and considerably less likely to kill a stranger over some fancied slight. Not that Bill Hilton had been a weakling, far from it. He'd just taken a little more time to turn matters over in his mind before reaching for his gun.

Mercador's chief worry was that Tom Hilton would somehow find a way to blame him for his brother's death and shoot him out of hand. Nor was this an exaggerated fear; Hilton had killed men for a good deal less than that. After thinking it over for a few minutes, Mercador rode back again in the direction from which he had come.

When he had got a half mile further back from the town, Mercador found a little copse of trees. There didn't seem to be anybody around so he dismounted and walked with his horse in among the trees and then tethered the mare to a low-hanging branch. He wasn't overly keen on the course of action which he was about to take, but it surely beat being gunned down by Tom Hilton.

Now during his military career, Mercador had seen more men killed by blood poisoning than any other cause. Sometimes, even a tiny scratch could turn septic and bring about a man's death, if some piece of crap or other got into the wound. For that reason, Mercador carefully rolled up his sleeve, so that he wouldn't end up with threads of filthy cotton being driven into the wound he was about to make. Then he drew his pistol, gritted his teeth and fired a glancing, superficial shot across the biceps of his left arm. It hurt like hell, far more than he had expected. Sometimes in the heat of battle, one might scarcely notice a trifling wound of this sort until things had quietened down a little. Receiving the same injury cold-bloodedly in the still of this little wood, with nothing to distract his attention was something else again. There was surprisingly little blood; the ball having just grazed a shallow groove, taking off the top few layers of skin and bruising the muscle which lay beneath. To make the whole thing look perfectly authentic, Mercador then fired another shot through the sleeve of his shirt, in a position roughly corresponding to the wound on his upper arm.

Once he'd rolled down his sleeve again, Mercador flexed his muscles a couple of times, causing the blood to start flowing from the injury and staining his shirt sleeve. He toyed briefly with the notion of inflicting a similarly artistically staged bullet wound to his horse, but decided against it. Instead, he saddled up and headed back to Indian Creek, composing in his head the story that he was going to spin to Tom Hilton.

★   ★   ★

The road towards El Paso ran through gently undulating country, with hills and woods visible here and there in the distance. There was no sign that Talbot Rogers could discern of either Fort Williams nor any other settlement. He walked on ahead of the others a little, with George Littlechild, who seemed a sensible enough fellow and probably closest in age to Talbot himself.

'What do you reckon,' asked Talbot, 'you think we're liable to come across any town between here and Fort Williams?'

'Couldn't say,' replied the other. 'Can't say as I know the land hereabouts. I guess we could sleep out in the open at a pinch.'

'Might have to. It'll be coming on dark in another hour. If we don't see any sign of life soon, I'm minded to call a halt and we can get off the road to find shelter.'

Littlechild shot the man walking along at his side a strange look and said, 'Shelter from what? You mean wolves and such?'

'Not exactly,' said Talbot.

After they had been travelling along for another ten minutes, Talbot stopped and announced that they would be moving off the road and seeking shelter for the night in a rocky bluff which towered away to the right, perhaps two or three miles from the road.

'Can't we just set down here?' asked young Hogan.

'That's not a smart move,' said Talbot, without giving any reasons or offering any sort of explanation.

'Why not?' said Tim Hogan. 'Seems mad to add so much to our journey. 'Sides, suppose some stage came by in the night or troop o' cavalry or something like that? We might find help that way. What for you think we should be hiding up in those rocks?'

Talbot Rogers shrugged indifferently and said, 'If you people want to take my advice, you'll come off away from this road and hunker down on that bluff.'

'Young fellow's got a point,' observed George Littlechild. 'Can't you tell us why you want us to trudge all the way over yonder?'

If there hadn't been women involved and it had just been a question of abandoning a bunch of men, Talbot wouldn't have bothered to say a word. He would simply have walked off and left those who wished to sleep right there, to their own devices and made off alone. He knew though that he couldn't behave so on this occasion, not if it meant placing the girl and the two grown women in hazard. He sighed, for he was a man who loathed and detested having to explain his motives.

'My current job is acting as a representative of the Colt Firearms company in Hertford, Connecticut,' said Talbot, 'but that's what you might term a recent development. For better than fifteen years, I worked for the provost marshals' department.'

'That some kind o' law?' asked one of the boys who had been riding the roof of the stage.

'Something of the sort. Military police. Keeping order in the army and tracking down offenders.'

'Where does that lead us?' asked Tim Hogan, an aggressive edge to his voice. Talbot understood this to mean that he was nursing a grievance for having been ticked off about his attentions to young Melanie. Now that he was in a group of men once more and others seemed to support his view of the case, Hogan was full of beans again. 'In the main, my job was tracking down fugitives,' explained Talbot patiently, 'men who were fleeing from some wrongdoing. I don't like to blow my own bugle, but I was good. The best, if I'm truthful. Nobody ever caught me napping and I always found the man I was looking for. Found them and brought them back.' He paused and then went on. 'Early on in the game, I found that I had some kind of a sense for when danger threatened. I couldn't explain it all to you folks, even if we had the time and leisure to sit here for a spell. Which, by the by, we don't. But I can tell you right now, there's a storm cloud heading our way and if we don't get off the road right this minute, you are all liable to be struck by the lightning.'

When Talbot Rogers had finished speaking, there was a deathly silence and then, without any more ado, the others began sheepishly moving off in the direction which he had indicated that they should go. Only young Tim Hogan was apparently dissatisfied about this turn of events, remarking to the man who had been involved in the shooting from the roof of the stage, 'Sounds to me like a gallon of hogwash in a pint pot!' The wounded man made no reply to this observation, being concerned only with the throbbing pain from the wound in his leg.

* * *

Back in Indian Creek, the interview with Tom Hilton that Mercador had so been dreading went more smoothly than he could have dared hope. Naturally, Ramon Mercador had not revealed that after shooting the horses, he had left the ambush to Bill Hilton and the other three. In the version of events which he had spun for Tom Hilton and the other eight remaining members of the gang, Mercador had rode down from the hills to join in the attack on the stage. There had been the fiercest gun battle imaginable, with hot lead flying through the air like it might have been a hailstorm. Only when he had seen his four companions fall in battle and it was clear that they were hopelessly outgunned had he fled the scene.

Tom Hilton watched him narrowly

while he was telling this tale, his eyes running over Mercador. When the story was ended, Hilton said nothing for a space and then shrugged, as though the thing was of little import. He said, 'You played your part. I would have turned and rode off myself, had I been there. How's your arm?'

'Hurtin'.'

'You want to get a doctor?'

'Hell, no!' exclaimed Mercador. 'I taken worse than that and never needed no sawbones.' Hilton nodded and the matter was ended. Ramon Mercador felt giddy and weak with relief. He had more than half expected Tom Hilton to shoot him down in a fury for coming back alive. He had a sudden and overpowering urge to visit the outhouse. Having the fear of death abruptly lifted from one did strange things to a man's bowels.

The ten members of the gang had strolled out to the edge of town; the better to talk privately. Although the sun had sunk below the horizon, it wasn't yet truly dark. The evening star was twinkling low in the dark blue sky and in another half hour it would be nightfall. Hilton said, 'What state was the stage in when you left, Mercador? Fit to travel?'

'I shot two of the horses. They might limp along for a while with four.'

'Where's the next stop?'

'Not for a way south,' said one of the other men. 'Little place called Green-haven. Two-bit little berg, maybe six houses in the whole town.'

'And after that?' asked Tom Hilton thoughtfully.

'Nothing 'til Fort Williams.'

Nobody said anything, waiting until they saw which way their leader's thoughts were running. At length, Hilton said, 'There's no point haring after them in the dark. We leave at first light tomorrow. If we don't take 'em on the road, then we'll maybe find them in this little town. Either way's fine by me.'

'I don't rightly understand . . . '

began one of the men, only to move back a pace or two when Hilton turned on him savagely.

'Don't understand, hey, you son of a bitch? Then I'll spell it out plain. My brother's dead and I'll have blood for it. I don't know which o' them on that stage fired the shot, so we'll kill the whole boilin' lot of 'em. That clear enough for you?'

It was certainly clear enough to all those present that they would be well-advised not to get crosswise to Tom Hilton in this matter and there were hasty nods and grunts of assent, all meant to indicate that what was all right for Tom Hilton was just fine and dandy for them as well. If Hilton wished to ride out the next day and murder everybody from a stagecoach, then none of them were about to gainsay him. The man who looked the least enthusiastic about the scheme was Ramon Mercador. He was racking his brains fearfully, praying that the lies he had fed to Hilton were not about to come back to haunt him.

* * *

By the time they reached the bluff and
had climbed up a little way until they
were out of sight of the road, everybody
was tired and irritable. The only one
who showed no signs of impatience or
annoyance about the enterprise was
Talbot. He had brought these people to
safety and that was what he had
intended to do. He neither expected,
nor especially wanted, their gratitude. It
was enough for him that he had done
his duty.

'This high enough?' enquired Tim
Hogan sarcastically. 'Sure you wouldn't
have us scramble up those rock-faces
and try to get to the top of that cliff
there?'

Talbot eyed the youngster, saying
mildly, 'No, I don't reckon that will be
needful. We're out of sight here and
that's all I desired.'

'Thank Christ for that!' muttered the
boy.

'No call for taking the Lord's name

in vain,' said Talbot, 'that ain't what I want to be hearing at all.'

They settled themselves down as best they were able. There was nowhere to tether the horses and so Talbot hobbled them, so that they wouldn't be able to wander too far in the night. He saw too that the ladies had the blankets and that water was doled out fairly. Then he announced, 'I'm taking first watch, say 'til eleven or thereabouts. Who'll take the next turn?'

There were no volunteers to relieve Talbot from his sentry duty at eleven and he shook his head in disgust, saying, 'You men ought to die o' shame. We got two ladies and a young girl to take care of here and none of you want to lend a hand. Well, so be it.'

As the others made themselves as comfortable as they could under the circumstances, Talbot clambered up to a rocky prominence overlooking the track along which they had come. He took out the long-barrelled pistol which he'd taken from his luggage and spun the cylinder to make sure that it was turning smoothly. He said to himself, 'You're a damned fool, Talbot, and no mistake. These folks ain't a morsel grateful to you for setting a watch over 'em. You might as well go straight to sleep yourself and that's a fact.' Despite these words, he knew very well that he would not be sleeping that night and that he would set up here on the rock, keeping an eye out for danger, while the others rested. By Talbot Rogers's lights, no real man ever allowed a lady to be in danger, not while he had breath in his body.

4

Of the ten men who were standing around by the corral shortly after dawn the next day, only one was keen on riding out on the vengeance trail. The other nine knew that Tom Hilton led them well enough on their exploits and that they did better with him than they were likely to do alone. For this reason, they were prepared to go along with him on this personal crusade, with the unspoken understanding that they would be rewarded in some way at some time in the future for their loyalty. This at any rate was the general feeling among eight of the men; Ramon Mercador was wondering if he would have done better to dig up and vanish the night before.

From all that Mercador was able to gather, Hilton's plan was for them to ride to where the ambush had taken place and then pick up the trail from there. He couldn't rightly recollect how things had looked after he ran off with his tail between his legs, but he surely hoped that there would be enough confusion and disorder when they reached the spot, that nothing would be seen to arouse Tom Hilton's suspicions. One thing was certain. If Hilton suspected for a moment that Mercador had been snoozing out of the way while his brother was fighting for his very life, then he would snuff out Mercador's life with no more compunction than he would feel in extinguishing a candle.

The Hilton Gang had been killing time in Indian Creek before heading south through Texas towards the Mexican border. Every year, things became neater and more orderly in the United States and with the increasing order came better organized law enforcement. Even a couple of years ago, there were whole swathes of territory from Kansas down as far south as Louisiana, where you could be nigh-on sure to find a fair sized town without a sheriff or marshal to be found within two days' ride. Sometimes there might be a vigilance committee to be wary of, but no regular law at all to speak of.

Times were changing though and more and more of even the smallest settlements were becoming civilized, with lawmen patrolling the streets and even telegraph wires linking them to nearby cities. Slowly but surely, bad men were being forced west and south if they wanted to be able to ride free and do as they pleased. The Hiltons and their boys had been heading south when they hit Indian Creek and it had seemed such a welcoming little town that they had lingered on until the ill-fated attack on the Butterfield mail.

'How far'd you say it was to where my brother died?' Hilton asked Mercador, as they saddled up.

'Maybe twenty, thirty miles,' answered the other vaguely.

'Well, which is it,' said Hilton irritably, 'twenty or thirty? Shit, you spent long enough as a soldier, if all you say is true. Happen you should be able to gauge a distance within a mile or two.'

'At least twenty, maybe a couple o' miles more.'

'That's more like it. See now, you can ride alongside of me as we go.'

Seldom had Ramon Mercador received an invitation which he felt more like declining, but it would have been madness to refuse. Smiling in a sickly fashion, he said, 'Sure thing, Tom.'

*   *   *

By the time Tom Hilton and his boys were in the saddle, the passengers from the mail coach had already been on the road for the best part of an hour. Sitting up all night, watching the occasional shooting star had been mighty lonely work for Talbot Rogers and as soon as he caught the first gleam of false dawn on the eastern horizon, he awakened the others and urged them to get ready to move out.

There was considerable reluctance on

the part of those Talbot woke up, to start off so early.

'Ah heck,' moaned George Little-child, the farmer, 'surely we don't have to leave this early?'

'Well, but we do,' replied Talbot politely, but with great firmness. 'We have to leave this very minute.'

So it was that at the time that Tom Hilton and his boys were setting out from Indian Creek, Talbot Rogers was saying to Littlechild, who was once again walking alongside him, ''less my eyes deceive me, I'd say that's a town ahead of us.'

'Your eyes are sharper than mine,' said the farmer, 'I'm blessed if I can see anything as might be a town.'

'You see that peak up yonder,' said Talbot, 'right on the horizon?'

'Just about. What of it?'

'There's a windpump sticking up just to the right of that rock. See it?'

The sun had barely risen and the light still uncertain. Littlechild shook his head and said, 'You may be right.'

'I'm right enough,' said Talbot. 'The wonder of it is that I didn't see it yesterday when we stopped for the night.'

A half hour later and most of the others could see what Talbot had already marked, that there was a huddle of buildings about two miles away. It looked to be a little hamlet, but all the weary men and women were thinking that at the very least they might be able to obtain food, drink and shelter in such a place. Nobody, having heard of their misfortunes, would be likely to turn them away empty-handed.

Talbot Rogers was as pleased as any of them to think that they were approaching somewhere which would provide for the travellers with which he had burdened himself. After the previous night, when not one single man had offered to take a turn at look-out duty with him, it had convinced Talbot that these were the most ungrateful set of fools he had had to deal with in a good long while.

As they came closer to the little town, Talbot Rogers began to think that his stewardship of the band was drawing to an end. He had not forgotten the urgency of the quest which he had agreed to undertake for the man from the Bureau of Indian Affairs. It was all well and good saving a dozen people from the wreck of that mail coach, but what if the delay spelled death for all those hundreds of people living in the homesteads and villages between here and El Paso? The sooner he had rid himself of his charges, the better for all concerned.

★ ★ ★

It took something over an hour for the ten riders to reach the scene of the previous day's ambush and when they did, they stumbled upon a vision of hell. The seven bodies which had been laying out in the wild overnight had provided good sustenance for various predators; chief among them the coyotes which lived in these parts. Not one of the corpses had escaped unscathed. Some had lost fingers and noses; two had lost entire arms, when two rival gangs of the wild dogs had fought tug o' war with the bodies of Carson and Bill Hilton. The members of the Hilton gang were by no means squeamish or sensitive types, but the sight of the chewed and mutilated bodies of their former comrades was a shocking one, even for such men as they.

Tom Hilton dismounted and wandered about the scene, staring at this and that, occasionally shooting an ill-favoured glance at Ramon Mercador. He examined one or two of the corpses closely and at last came back to where his men were sitting on their horses, waiting. Not one of them had felt the need to dismount and see at close quarters the evidence of mortality lying strewn around the dusty ground which lined the roadway.

'I don't see any horses,' remarked

Hilton, fixing Mercador with an accusatory eye, 'not one.'

One of the men said, 'Happen those from the stage took the horses with 'em when they left.'

'Yes,' said Tom Hilton, 'so I thought. But what about the dead ones?'

'Dead ones?' asked Mercador. 'What dead ones? Why should any of the horses have been killed?'

'Why? I'll tell you for why, you lying whoreson, because in a gun battle with five men on horseback attacking a coach, like you said you and the others did, everybody on that coach'd be aiming at the horses, not just the riders. Bigger targets. You know that, well as I do. You all know it. Yet there's not a single horse to be seen.'

The sun had barely been up for an hour and it was still chilly, but Ramon Mercador was sweating. He could feel beads of cold liquid running down his chest and was uncomfortably aware that sweat was gathering too on his forehead. He tried to bluster his way out of it, saying, 'How the hell do I know what happened to the horses? I didn't stop to see what was happening.' He realized that he had made a slip and tried to retreat. 'Leastways, I didn't stop 'til I saw that everybody had been shot.'

'And not one horse, hey?' asked Hilton. 'How far were the boys when they was shot, answer me that?'

'How far? Hell, I couldn't say. Fifty yards, thirty yards, what does it matter?'

'I'll show you,' said Hilton. 'Get down from your horse now and come over here.'

'Who, me?'

'Yes, you. Come on, Mercador, you've some explaining to do.'

None of the others said anything and it looked to Mercador as though he was alone in this. Nobody was apt to cross Tom Hilton when he was in such a mood. He dismounted and went over to where Hilton was standing. 'Well then, what is it?'

'Come here.' Hilton beckoned for

Mercador to follow him and led him to where the body of Abe Wilson lay. Wilson had been a particular friend of Mercador's and he had been grieved at the man's death. When he reached the body, Tom Hilton crouched down by it and pointed at the face. 'Notice anything here?' he asked.

The dead man's face presented an unappetizing spectacle. One ear had been chewed away by some animal and the open, staring eyes seemed to Mercador to be full of reproach. The ear had streams of dried blood leading from it, besmirching the corpse's cheek.

'Looks to me like he was shot,' said Mercador. 'Like I said, there was a shoot-out. What d'you expect to see?'

'I don't look to find powder burns around a wound received at thirty yards' distance, for one thing,' remarked Hilton in a soft and deadly voice. 'Wilson was shot up close, whoever killed him must have had the weapon at point-blank range. How do you explain it?'

Despite the cold feeling in the pit of

his stomach, Mercador swore under his breath and said angrily, 'I can't explain it. There was a heap o' shooting and when I saw we was outnumbered, I rode like hell. What would you have done? Up and out with it, what do you say I've done?'

Tom Hilton smiled slightly, not at all sorry that the other man's dander was up. 'You want I should spell it out? Here it is then. I say you took out the lead horses on that stage, like you've done before. Then I'm guessing you let the others, my damned brother included, do the dangerous work. I think that somethin' went wrong and they were all shot when they were off their horses. While you sat on your arse, halfway up a hill.'

It was hard to imagine a more succinct and accurate summation of the events of the previous day and for once in his life, Ramon Mercador was utterly lost for words. This did not pass unremarked by Tom Hilton, who was narrowly watching the other man and saw the fear and guilt in his eyes. 'Yes,' he said, 'it's just as I reckoned. Bill's blood is on your hands and you'll answer now for his death.'

It was no more than Mercador had expected. Very slowly, he turned to face Tom Hilton squarely and said, 'If you'll have it so.'

There was not the least delay in Hilton's actions. The words had scarcely passed Mercador's lips than Tom Hilton pulled his pistol and shot the other man down like a dog. Ramon Mercador hadn't even enough time to reach for his gun. As he lay in the dust, his eyes glazing over, Hilton walked over to him and landed a vicious kick, right in his face. Then he spat on the prone man, saying, 'That's for my brother!'

★   ★   ★

In 1857, when New Yorker John Butterfield was awarded the contract to run a mail coach service linking St Louis in Missouri with San Francisco, his first action was to establish 141 stage posts. These were places where a staff of men made sure that fresh horses were ready when the coaches came in and had the means to make minor repairs to the Celerity and Concord coaches that Butterfield was using for his mail service to California. Some of these stage posts were in cities. Others were in one-horse towns like Greenhaven.

Precisely thirty-seven people lived in Greenhaven; twenty-five of whom farmed the fields which surrounded the town and hemmed it in on all sides. Of the other dozen, two ran the smithy, which catered for passing trade, as well as fixing broken ploughshares and suchlike. Two more ran a tiny store and trading post, one was retired and lived on his savings and another two men worked for Butterfield's, running the stage post.

When Talbot and his companions trudged into town, a little before eight in the morning, there was some consternation. Those living in the community, being in the main farmers, were early risers. The first man they encountered, a ruddy-faced man with a hoe over his shoulder, stopped dead in his tracks to stand and stare.

'I'm guessing you all are from the mail coach as was expected yesterday?'

'That's the fact of the matter,' replied Talbot Rogers. 'These people are sorely in need of food and drink. Maybe you could help us to find vittles and shelter?'

The man thought about this for a moment, before suggesting that they carry on down the street to where the Butterfield's people had their place.

Dave Starret and William Masters, the two men in charge of the stage post, were most surprised to see the gaggle of men, women and horses arrive at the barn that had been tricked out by Butterfield's as a stopping place for their coaches.

'Holy Moses!' exclaimed Starret. 'You surely ain't the passengers off the stage bound for Fort Williams?'

'That we are, son,' said Talbot, 'and

I'm hoping as your company has some provision to make for folk such as them. If not, then the good Lord alone knows what's to become of them.'

It took a while to explain what had happened and when Starret and Masters realized that there had been a raid on the stage, they looked very grim and exchanged meaningful glances. William Masters shook his head and said, 'What did I tell you 'bout those bearer bonds? Isn't it that I told you somebody was apt to catch wind of what was being carried?' Suddenly he brightened up and asked the weary crowd, 'Say, I don't suppose any of you good people happened to think to bring the mail sack along of you?'

Talbot Rogers, who was in a rare hurry to be on his way to Fort Williams, cut in at this point, saying, 'I told them not to burden themselves with anything, even their own bags. What's all this foolishness about mail sacks?'

'Oh don't set any more mind to it,' said Masters hastily, 'it's just that there was some valuable documents being carried. It can't be helped.'

'Here's the way of it, son,' explained Talbot patiently, 'I have to be on my way. It's a matter of life or death and I won't be delayed further. I've brought these people here and as far as I can make out, your company should be taking care of them from here on in. That's all and I don't aim to have a long debate about it, either.'

Taken aback by the firm tone in which Talbot spoke and his air of not being a man used to having his wishes crossed, both Masters and Starret hastened to assure him that the Butterfield's company would do all in their power to look after these unfortunate victims of robbery. It was while they were smoothing things over to the best of their ability that there came a single shot, which blew away half of Clarence Barker's head and caused him to fall dead on the spot. His daughter Melanie, being liberally spattered with blood and brain matter, began to shriek hysterically.

Mercador's death passed almost without note by the eight men sitting on their horses, watching to see what Tom Hilton would do to avenge his dead brother. It has to be said that Ramon Mercador had not been the most popular man in the gang and several men had observed before his tendency to stay clear of danger after demonstrating his prowess with a rifle. That his skulking out of the way like that had now led to his sudden and untimely death at Hilton's hands did not strike anybody as especially surprising or undeserved. They were a good deal less enthusiastic, though, about chasing after the passengers from the stage in order to massacre them. This was especially the case after they had recollected the rumour which had led to Bill Hilton and the other four setting out to ambush the mail coach in the first place.

After Ramon Mercador had been

shot down like the mangy dog that many of them believed him to be, there was a few seconds' quiet. Even a skunk like Mercador deserved a certain respect after death.

Nobody spoke for all of ten seconds, until one of the men, Pete Jackson by name, said, 'What d'you all think happened to those bearer bonds o' which we heard tell? Reckon as those folk took 'em with 'em when they dug up and left?'

'Now there's a thought,' said Tom Hilton appreciatively. 'Thank the Lord one of us has the sense God gave a goat. Some of you take a look under that tarp.'

Nothing loath, three of the riders dismounted and went round to the back of the stage. There, beneath the boxes, trunks and portmanteaus of the passengers, they found what they were looking for. The mail sack was padlocked at the top, but the canvas was not proof against a determined assault with a razor-sharp Bowie knife. Once it had been gutted like a fish, they tipped the contents out into the dust.

There, among the letters, were three large, official looking packages. They were all three of them addressed to the bank in El Paso.

'Open 'em up, boys,' cried Tom Hilton jovially, 'let's see what we got.'

What they had was $3500 worth of bearer bonds.

'Shit,' said the man who had hacked open the mail sack, 'that works out at . . . '

He tried in vain to divide $3,500 by nine. One of the others accomplished the task by figuring a tenth part of the sum, which was considerably easier than a calculation involving a division by nine.

'It's better than $350 each.'

'What are we waitin' for? Let's get to some town and turn these'un into cash money!'

'Yeah, let's make tracks . . . '

Tom Hilton's voice cut across their rejoicing. He said, 'We're going nowhere and doing nothing 'til I settled scores with the man who killed my brother.'

There was an uncomfortable silence. After all, Bill hadn't been their brother, but some innate delicacy prevented any of them from putting the matter into such plain terms. Either a rare delicacy or perhaps because they had just seen Tom Hilton gun down one man and not one of them had any inclination to get crosswise to their boss when he was in such a mood as this.

Tom Hilton cast his eyes around the eight men and gauged their innermost feelings most accurately. He said, 'I ain't 'bout to force any one o' you to come alongside o' me on this. But I'll tell you this for nothing. Any man as rides away now is stone dead to me. Is that clear?'

5

All of the men who had been riding with the Hilton brothers were tough enough individuals and not given to allowing others to shove them around. Nevertheless, they all knew that there was strength in numbers and that if you wished to set up as a road agent or knock over a bank or anything of that kind, then you were better doing it in the company of one or two like-minded fellows, rather than by your own self.

Once you pick up with a few others, then unless you're after endless squabbling and a life of long, pointless arguments, you needs must have one man who is the leader and makes the final choice in matters. The Hiltons had been natural leaders of the gang and now that Bill Hilton was gone, it was only natural that the remaining brother should take charge. The question was though, how far were the others prepared to follow Hilton? There was little profit for any of them to be found in chasing after a bunch of strangers and shooting them down because one of them might have put a bullet through Bill Hilton's head. Still, they each of them had now the equivalent of $350 or more and once he'd wrought his revenge, Tom Hilton would certainly come up with other profitable schemes, same as he always had. In the end, all nine of them thought it better to stay with the gang than take their chances alone.

Following the trail of the men and women who had abandoned the stage and set off towards Fort Williams required no great art. The track was poached up all over, by horses, and men and women's feet both. When Hilton and the others reached the point where the travellers had headed off to the bluff for the night, they didn't bother to follow the tracks in that direction. They could see that a second set of tracks led back to the road and worked out easily enough that those they were following had just spent the night up in the rocks.

'Anybody know around here particular well?' asked Tom Hilton.

'I been this way afore,' said one of the men, 'there's a little hamlet called Greenhaven up ahead.'

'How far?'

'Few miles. Should make it in less'n an hour.'

So it was that forty-five minutes later, Hilton and his men sat at their ease, watching the little town into which they were about to ride. The first thing they noticed was that there was some species of hullabaloo going on around a large barn on the edge of town. So busy were folk clustering round the scene, that not one of them had noticed the nine riders who had reined in some 400 yards from the town. To Tom Hilton, this looked to be the ideal moment to start teaching those who had murdered his brother the error of their ways and so he slid the carbine out from the scabbard at the front of the saddle, took general aim at the group of men and women standing around the barn and let fly at once.

Talbot Rogers reacted quicker than any of the others to the shot which killed young Melanie's father. The echo had barely faded, when he had grabbed hold of the girl's dress and unceremoniously dragged her to the ground. Then he shouted urgently to the rest of the crowd, who were standing around looking quite at a loss, 'Get yourselves into the barn! Hurry, now!' He had no more idea than anybody else who was shooting, but that didn't matter all that much. The main thing was to get out of sight of the gunman, whoever he might be.

After calling his warning to the others, Talbot manhandled the frightened girl into the barn, half dragging and half shoving her, making sure that they kept as low as could be. There were no other shots.

Once everybody was safely in the barn, Talbot drew his pistol and ventured to peep through a crack in the rough wooden wall. He saw a dozen or so riders, sitting on their horses and staring in the direction of the barn. He had not the least notion who they might be, but could tell that they meant mischief. The riders were a pretty nondescript bunch to look at, the only bright colour to be seen was a scarlet bandana around the neck of one of the men. Other than that, they were a dusty, travel-stained crew by the look of them. The girl, far from resenting his rough handling of her, seemed to regard Talbot as a pillar of strength. She huddled near him, obviously finding comfort and a feeling of safety in his presence.

One of the Butterfield's men came over to Talbot and said, 'Any idea what's to do, sir?'

'Not in the least,' he replied, slightly irritated that everybody appeared to take it as a matter of course that he would know more than they about any situation. 'Some business rival of yours, perhaps?'

'I don't think so . . . ' began the young man, before realizing that the question had not been meant seriously. He said, 'We got rifles in the office. You think as I should break 'em out?'

'Depends how attached you are to this life. I'd say that we might be about to fight for our lives.'

As it happened, Talbot was quite wrong about this, for as he watched, the band of riders abruptly whirled round and made off away from the town at a fair lick. The danger appeared to be over.

'Stay in here, you folk,' he told the others who were huddled against the walls of the barn, making sure that they couldn't be seen from outside. 'I'm going to see what's what.'

There was no mystery about the rapid disappearance of the men who had begun firing at them, because once Talbot was standing in the road which passed through Greenhaven on the way to Fort Williams, he saw at once that a body of men were coming on towards the town. Even though they were a good mile away, Talbot was able to see that they were all wearing blue and that they were travelling as a compact and well-ordered group. If they ain't cavalry, thought Talbot to himself, then I'm a Dutchman.

As it happened, Talbot Rogers was not a Dutchman and the riders who shortly rode into Greenhaven were indeed a troop of U.S. Cavalry from Fort Williams. It seemed likely that the men who had taken a shot at the passengers from the mail coach had spotted the approaching troops and decided to hightail it away from the town. The young captain in charge of the men didn't find the news of the shooting to be all that interesting. He certainly showed no inclination to go chasing off after the killers of Clarence Barker.

'I'm sorry and all,' said the officer,

'but we've important business away north. Need a little shoeing done, if your smith can oblige. Other than that, we'll not be lingering hereabouts.'

Talbot toyed with the idea of handing over the letter which Carson had entrusted to him. The dead man had, though, been most insistent about the need for the missive to be placed only in the hands of the officer commanding at Fort Williams. Besides which, these men were heading away from the fort. Talbot apprehended that there was some urgency in the matter. Now that he had seen these people safely here and there were a bunch of soldiers around, he felt that he could decently leave them to their own devices.

As he moved from person to person, saying a few words here and there, Talbot was uncomfortably aware that the girl Melanie was sticking to him like a cocklebur. He felt that he should perhaps condole with her on the death of her father, but hardly knew the right words to do so. Happen one of the ladies will take her under their wing, he thought hopefully. His aim was not to make a big announcement about his departure, but simply to slip quietly away when folk were otherwise occupied and leave without even bidding any of them farewell. The only fly in that particular ointment was the young girl who would not leave his side. When he sidled over to his horse, or rather the horse which he had commandeered back at the site of the ambush, Talbot found that the girl still had no evident intention of letting him leave. It was, he decided, time for some plain speaking.

'Look, Miss . . . ' he began.

'Oh, please don't call me Miss,' said the girl, 'it makes me feel old. Just Melanie will do fine.'

'Miss Melanie,' said Talbot, 'I know you won't be offended, but I have to leave now. I know you've had a terrible loss and I'm sorry for it, but I have business to attend to.'

'Loss?' said the girl. 'Oh, you mean my pa. Truth to tell, I didn't really know him. Not 'til a week or two back, anyways. Never got the chance to get to know him, as you might say.'

'That makes mighty strange listening,' Talbot said thoughtfully, rubbing his chin, 'but I don't have time to talk on it. Run along and tell your story to one of the ladies, there's a good girl.'

'You're going to Fort Williams, ain't you?'

'That I am.'

'Well then, I guess as it won't harm you none to have me ride along o' you. My pa has, had kin up that way. I don't know what'll become of me if I'm stuck here.'

She could see that Talbot was wavering and redoubled her efforts, saying, 'I feel safe with you, sir. I know you won't let nothing hurt me.'

'It's a two day ride from here. It would mean sleeping out another night.'

'I don't mind that. I've camped out with my cousins.'

It was very clear to Talbot Rogers

that if he delayed much longer then others would notice that he was heading off and then they too would ask to accompany him. If he just agreed to take this child with him, he might yet be able to slip off without any fuss.

'This is ad . . . I mean to say deuce of a nuisance,' he said irritably, 'can't you attach yourself to some other individual? I'm surely not one to play nursemaid to you.'

The girl looked so crestfallen to be spoken to thus, that Talbot felt ashamed. She had, after all, come within a whisker of being raped and then seen several people shot dead, including her own father. It was a hell of a thing for her to go through and she only fifteen years of age. He said, 'Oh, very well. Fetch your horse over here, without making a production of it and we'll just go off quietly.'

'Thank you,' she said, a broad grin splitting her face, 'thank you so much!'

As Talbot had figured, there was so much fuss and talking going on between the passengers from the stage, the folk living in the town and the troopers from the fort, that nobody noticed the two of them leading their horses off. When they were a hundred yards or so from the barn, Talbot said, 'Well, mount up then and we'll be off.'

As they trotted south, Talbot thought over one last time the possibility that he had any sort of responsibility either to care further for his fellow passengers from the mail coach or to tell them of his impending departure. Try as he might, he couldn't see that he owed any of those people a thing.

Once they were fairly on their way, Talbot thought that he should ask the child a little about herself, maybe comfort her a little, seeing as she had had a pretty bad time of it lately. Before he could say anything though, Melanie Barker herself spoke.

'How come you stopped being a lawman?' she asked. 'Didn't you like it any more?'

Talbot turned and looked at the girl. She was the first person in a good, long while who had asked him that question straight out like that. He thought for a space and then said slowly, 'I don't know as I'd say I didn't like it any more. I was good at it and it was never really work for me. Riding out alone, answerable to nobody. It was a good life.'

'You weren't answerable to anybody?' she asked in surprise. 'I thought this was an army thing?'

'Well, so it was. But they gave me my head, as you might say. The officer above me, he knew that if he let me be, I'd bring back the man I went after. They kind of let me get on with it.'

'So why'd you stop?'

'For a young person, you're mighty pressing. Here's the way of it. Most all those I went in search of were wanted on the capital charge. Murderers, rapists and such. You know what I mean by the capital charge?'

She shook her head.

'Means that when they fetched up before the court martial, they was liable to draw a death sentence. Mostly hanging, sometimes shooting. As arresting officer, it was my duty to attend the executions. After some years, I'd seen enough men die like that and so I left the army.'

The girl didn't say anything for the next few minutes and when the silence looked as though it was going to stretch on uncomfortably long, Talbot said, 'So how come you didn't know your pa that well?'

She shrugged. 'He left my ma when I was too little to remember him. Went off with another woman. Some time since, Ma and me'd been scrapping like cat and dog and one day, he just turns up on the doorstep.'

'What did you and your mother fight over?'

'Nothing special. When I could put up my hair, some boy I wanted to go on a picnic with. Just things.'

'So where did your pa fit into the scheme?'

'He told Ma that he wanted to get to

know me. Said he'd got himself a new job away over in El Paso. They kind of agreed that I could go live with him for a spell. Ma'd had about enough o' me by then and so told him he was welcome to me.'

Talbot thought about this and then said, 'So how did you get along with him?'

'All right, I guess. I never set eyes on him 'til two weeks since, so I never had a chance to get to know him real good. But I recollect as he told me that his mother lived nigh to Fort Williams.'

The landscape through which the two of them were riding was monotonous and bleak. It wasn't desert, but the land was arid and the only vegetation sparse and scrubby.

Although Talbot was a solitary-minded individual, he observed that young Melanie was bright and lively enough and would probably be apt to liven up the journey to some extent. He had in his time had to endure travelling companions who were a sight duller than this child and so he thought that all things considered, the next few days might not be so bad.

* * *

There was no percentage in tangling with the cavalry and so Hilton and his men rode off fast, as soon as they realized the significance of the column of men heading into the little town. There was no special reason to expect pursuit, but the nine riders, nevertheless, kept up a pretty lively pace for half an hour or so. They were up and into the hills surrounding the town before they reined in and took breath to see what might be done next.

A backward glance or two told Hilton and his boys that nobody was coming after them and they then fell to debating their next course of action.

'Seems to me,' said one man, 'we want to get to the nearest big town and cash those there bonds. Can't speak for the rest o' you, but I ain't 'xactly what

101

you'd call flush.'

There were murmurs of agreement to this. Out of the corner of their eyes, the eight men watched Tom Hilton, so as to get some clue about the way his mind was moving. Hilton, though, said nothing and his face betrayed no indication of what he was thinking. It was during this awkward silence that they heard the sound of a body of horsemen heading towards them from the opposite direction to that from which they had come. A rocky outcrop reared up and blocked their view in that direction, but they didn't have long to wait, because round the edge of the rocky bluff came a troop of Indians. These fellows all looked to be armed to the teeth and it was not at first clear which of the groups was the larger. That being so, Hilton's band at once drew and cocked their weapons, so as to be prepared for any eventuality.

The Indians gave the impression of being surprised to find anybody up in the hills and they came to a halt twenty yards away from the other men. The two groups sat there on their horses, eyeing each other warily. Although the white men had a slight advantage, in that their guns were ready and cocked, it was only a slender one, because there were at least fifteen or twenty Indians in total. If shooting started, it was likely to be a bloody affair. Fortunately, it never came to this point. One of the men riding with Hilton was a 'breed who called himself Ben. This man was a taciturn and short tempered individual who had been in a number of brawls precipitated by men making remarks about his ancestry. None of the others knew what tribe, if any he belonged to, but he seemingly recognized something about the Indians in front of them, for he said, 'You men put up your weapons. I'm a goin' to parlay with 'em.'

The man they knew as Ben trotted his horse forward, until he was barely six feet in front of the lead rider of the Indian party. Then he halted and began, as it seemed to the others, to wave his arms around and grunt unintelligibly. This went on for long enough for the others to begin feeling uneasy. Then it was over and Ben wheeled round and rode back to them. The Indians approached and one or two of the men raised their weapons in readiness for action.

Ben said urgently, 'Chris'sake, you fools! Let 'em be. They got no argument with us.'

It appeared that the 'breed was right, because the fifteen riders simply walked their horses past the white men and then, once they were clear, urged their mounts on into a trot. Then they were gone.

'What was that all about?' asked Tom Hilton, a mite irritated that somebody other than he had played the leading role in settling some difficulty.

'Good news for us,' said Ben, 'those boys was carrying guns that we sold 'em one time. They 'membered me, at any rate. You white men all look alike to them, though. Don't you recall, 'bout six months since? We had a crate or two of guns and we traded 'em to the Indians. Those boys were carrying those self-same guns.'

'Well, ain't that worked out a treat,' said Hilton, a broad smile splitting his face. 'It's just like it says in scripture. You cast your bread upon the waters and it will return to you a hundred-fold. Praise the Lord!'

'Happen there's somewhat in that,' said Ben, 'but you ain't yet heard the best of it.'

'There's more?' asked one of the men.

'You bet your life there's more. More than you lunkheads can guess.'

Tom Hilton was getting tired of the 'breed putting on side and playing centre stage. He said, 'Well then, come on and out with it. You're as talkative as a woman sometimes. What else did you learn?'

Ben looked like the cat who'd got the cream and was by no means disposed to spill all at once. The look in Hilton's face, though, suggested that that gentleman would take it exceedingly ill if he were caused to wait much longer and so Ben announced grandly, 'Fact is, I'd say our fortunes are made. Leastways, we got it made for a space. Those boys are riding to some big gathering. They're Kiowa, but they're heading off to a feast with a bunch of Comanche too. It's scheduled for the full moon, two nights from now. Next day, they're risin'.'

'Risin'?' said Hilton. 'What are you talking of?'

'Just 'xactly what I say. They're going to be attacking Fort Williams and then when they taken all the guns there, they gonna sweep down through the country, killin' all the white men as they can lay their hands on.'

Now it was Tom Hilton's turn to smile. He said, 'Lord, I see just what you mean. Rich pickings for us, if we can avoid gettin' our throats cut. You're saying as we can just kind o' tag along after them and then take whatever we've a fancy to? No law, no soldiers.

Just help ourselves, is that it?'

'So I thought,' said Ben.

'You thought right, boy. I reckon as our luck's in.'

6

When they had set out, a little before midday, Talbot Rogers had estimated that the two of them should strike Fort Williams by late the following evening. His calculations were all founded upon travelling at a trot, interspersed, if the girl was up to it, with a little cantering. All his figuring though was set at naught within two hours.

After they had been riding at an easy pace for a half hour, Talbot noticed that the mare he had taken was breathing a little heavily and seemed to him to be making heavy weather of what was, after all, a smooth and level track. He said nothing for a while, but noticed that he was falling behind Melanie's horse. She called back at him cheerfully, 'Come on, you slowpoke!'

'Wait along there,' he said loudly, 'we needs must stop.'

The girl reined in and then turned her horse back to see what the problem was. While she was doing so, Talbot dismounted and began feeling the horse's belly carefully. His heart sank as he found one spot which was distended and the touching of which caused the beast to jitter sideways in distress.

'What is it?' said Melanie. 'Why have we stopped?'

'I couldn't take oath to it, but I'm strongly of the opinion that this creature of mine has the colic.'

'Colic? Are you sure?'

'Not yet. But we can't go any further just now.'

The girl got down from her own mount and came over to stroke the head of the horse that Talbot had been riding. She said quietly, 'I seed a horse with the colic. It was just terrible. Is there naught to be done?'

'Not here and now. Animal doctors can sometimes do stuff, but I wouldn't know how.'

'What can be done?'

'I seen a man once that kind of massaged a horse's belly and untwisted some part or other. Another time, one fellow I saw pushed a sharp spike in and released a lot of gas. We can't do anything of that sort.'

'What are we going to do then?'

'Just set here and wait for a bit.'

It took two hours for the horse that Talbot had been riding to become so mad with the pain of whatever was afflicting its entrails that it collapsed on the ground and began rolling around in agony, whinnying the while. The creature's eyes rolled in terror and flecks of foam appeared around its mouth. When matters reached that stage, Talbot told Melanie to take a stroll away from where they had stopped. The child seemed disposed to argue the point, but he was quite firm. She had got thirty yards when there was the report of a pistol. When she turned in alarm, it was to see that Talbot had put the creature out of its misery.

Talbot was not feeling any too chatty

after being compelled to put an end to the suffering animal. Nonetheless, Melanie Barker was determined to find out how this affected their plans. She said, 'Can't we just double up and both ride on the one horse?'

'Not for long, we can't. You can ride and I'll walk. But it's like to double our journey time to Fort Williams.'

'Hadn't we better start going then?'

The girl's spirit and pluck suddenly touched Talbot's heart and he reached out his hand and patted her on the head, saying, 'Lord, but you're a game one!'

She smiled and then said, 'Does that mean we're going on now?'

'I guess so.'

They carried on for the rest of that afternoon, taking it in turns to ride and walk. For his own part, Talbot would have been content to let Melanie ride for the whole time, but she wanted to stretch her legs from time to time and so insisted in getting off sometimes.

They hadn't much in the way of food

and what they did have was not overly appetizing, consisting just of dry bread and a hunk of cheese, the meagre fare being washed down with draughts of water from the canteen.

By about three in the afternoon, Melanie was growing weary and was plainly in need of a good long rest. Talbot was uneasy about stopping by the roadside, notwithstanding the fact that they had seen no other travellers on the road since setting off. It was while he was musing on what to do next, that he caught sight of a gleam of white in the distance, perhaps a mile and a half away and to the right of the direction in which they were making their way.

'Your eyes are younger than mine, sharper too most likely,' said Talbot. 'Look over yonder and tell me what you see.'

The girl squinted into the distance and said, 'You mean that little building over yonder?'

'It is a building, then? That's a mercy.

Think you're up to walking across a bit of rough ground now, 'til we reach it?'

Melanie shrugged. 'Looks like I'll have to.'

As the two of them drew close to the low, whitewashed structure, Talbot saw that it was a mission station. Judging by the cross atop of it and the shrine to Our Lady, which stood to one side, he guessed that it was run by Catholics. Before they reached the door, a black-robed man emerged and asked them their business.

'Just two travellers as could do with resting and perhaps a bite to eat,' replied Talbot. 'We mean you no harm.'

'Come in then,' said the priest, 'And a good welcome to you. Forgive me for being a little cautious. There's need, just now.'

The room into which they were led was cool and dark, the narrow slits of windows allowing little light to enter the place. Talbot guessed rightly that the purpose of such small windows was defensive, should the missioner have to hole up here against people seeking to harm him. When they were seated, the priest introduced himself.

'My name is Father O'Grady and I'm pleased to meet you both. Although why you're wandering across the territory in this way, the good Lord alone knows. Father and daughter, are you?'

'No,' said Talbot, 'we're no blood relations. I'm Talbot Rogers and this is Miss Barker. We're on our way to Fort Williams.'

'You'll be lucky to reach it alive, the way you're currently situated,' observed Father O'Grady dryly. 'What are you about, Mr Rogers, to take a young girl on such a perilous journey?'

'It's by way of being a long story. I don't suppose that you would be able to offer us some refreshments?'

Although they did not realize it as they tucked into the food which the priest set before them, the Hilton gang were only a few hours' ride from the mission station. Luckily, Tom Hilton and his men were not making their way in a straight line, either literally or metaphorically. The nine riders were weaving their way through the low range of hills which ran parallel to the road to Fort Williams and it was while they were picking their way along the rocky trail that a most unfortunate incident occurred.

There was not a great deal in the way of law enforcement in those parts of the territory at that time but every so often, a marshal or bounty hunter would show up in search of this or that individual. Hilton and the eight men riding with him rode round a pile of boulders and came upon three men who were brewing up coffee on a little fire built of dry branches from a nearby bristlecone pine. Although they must have heard the horses picking their way along the rocky path, the men crouching round the fire showed no signs of alarm at the sudden appearance of the nine riders.

'Hidy,' said the man holding the pot of coffee, 'fine day for a ride.' He continued fussing round with the pot, trying to position it more effectively on the rocks which surrounded the fire.

The fact that all three of the men round the fire were sporting tin stars did not escape the notice of any of the men in Hilton's party. Although they were not over-fond of lawmen, they had other fish to fry that day and would have been quite happy to carry on past and get about their business, if one of those warming his hands at the fire had not stood up, stared hard at them all, before focusing his attention on the one man of the group he seemingly recognized. He said, 'You be Tom Hilton, I reckon!'

The other two men looked up in surprise, mingled with interest and also alarm at the odds which they found themselves facing. Now Tom Hilton was usually very quick to start shooting, never troubling himself unduly about such minor matters as giving a man warning and affording him a chance to defend himself. This time, however, he met his match, because before he or any of his band had even moved, the fellow who had challenged him had drawn his pistol and had it pointing at Hilton's face. He said, 'Even if any o' your boys should draw on me now, I can promise you'll be dead before they get off a shot.'

It wasn't often that Hilton was quite lost for words, but it took him a second or two to come to terms with this unexpected turn of events. When he had done so, he said in a low voice, 'Don't any of you men pull your pistols. Just take it easy, you hear what I tell you?' Throughout this speech, he had never once taken his eyes off the face of the man who was drawing down on him. To this individual, he said, 'What will you have? We outnumber you nigh on three to one. It'll be a bloody business if we set to.'

So far the other two men — whether they were marshals or deputies, it was impossible to say without getting closer and examining their badges — had made no further move after getting to their feet. They hadn't drawn and it was likely that, just like Hilton's men, none of them wanted to do anything which might precipitate a bloodbath. That this was the case was shown when one of them said, addressing Hilton directly, 'Seems to me, Mister whatever your name is, that my partner here's got hisself into a muddle. He's mistook you for a fellow called Hilton. We heard of that man, but we ain't lookin' for him this minute. Fact is, we're after a horse of another colour.'

'I'm tellin' you,' said the fellow holding the gun on Hilton, 'this here's Tom Hilton. I'd know him anywhere!'

'Shut up, Dave,' said the other man easily, 'you made an error, is all. Happens to the best of us.' He turned to Tom Hilton again, saying, 'Tell you what, now. Why'nt you and your friends just ride on, nice and slow? We don't none of us want any bloodlettin', I wouldn't have thought.'

'What does you friend say?' enquired

118

Hilton. 'He of the same opinion?'

'Don't you mind him none. Just ride on, real slow, like.'

Keeping a weather eye on the man who still had a pistol pointing in his direction, Tom Hilton set his mount walking slowly forward, being sure to keep his hands perfectly still, so that nobody might have any apprehension that he was about to go for his gun. The other eight members of the party also started their horses, moving forward slowly, passing the three men standing round the fire. The one who had recognized Hilton wore a look of baffled fury on his face. He was in a minority of one though, because all the others, both the lawmen and the bandits, did not desire any sort of gun battle that afternoon.

Ten of the men up in those hills were happy with the peaceful outcome of the encounter that afternoon. The two exceptions were Tom Hilton and the man who had drawn his gun and aimed it right at Hilton's face. The deputy marshal was exceedingly ticked off because he had a crow to pluck with Hilton from long ago and thought he had a chance to take Hilton in charge and see him hang. As for Tom Hilton himself, no man had ever aimed a gun at him in that way and lived to brag about it later and Hilton was damned if this son of a bitch was going to be the exception to this rule.

The nine men on horseback were past the marshal and his deputies and everybody had begun to breathe a little easier. The man who had challenged Hilton had reluctantly returned his gun to its holster and was just on the point of sitting back down again, when Tom Hilton whirled round in the saddle, pulling the carbine from its scabbard at the same time. Then, before anybody knew what he was about, Hilton raised the weapon and put a ball straight through the head of the man who had had the temerity to threaten him. Having accomplished this, he dug his spurs savagely into the flanks of the mare and sent her skittering perilously along the rock-strewn and uncertain path.

As soon as their leader had fired, the others knew it was life or death and that if they didn't wish to catch a bullet in the back, then they had best dig up as fast as they were able. The whole body of riders went thundering along the track and it was a miracle that none of their mounts lost their footing. The two men they had left behind loosed off a half dozen shots at them, none of which hit anybody. There was no sign of pursuit. However angry those lawmen might have been, they weren't about to face down men when the odds had just lengthened to better than four to one.

*   *   *

Meantime, a few miles away at the Catholic mission station, Talbot Rogers and young Melanie Barker were having an altogether more peaceful and agreeable time. Father O'Grady was a good host and after he had established to his own satisfaction that these two people were not up to any mischief and were in need of shelter and sustenance, he relaxed a little and plied them with the choicest vittles at his disposal. Truth to tell, it was only a haunch of cold ham with cornpone, but Talbot and the girl were ravenously hungry after their long day's walk and they were glad of the food.

'In these parts,' explained the priest, 'the Indians call us the 'Cross God Men'. I mean me and my fellow Catholics, you understand. There's a Baptist mission down towards El Paso and they call them the 'Water God Men'. On account of their habit of dunking converts right under in the river, you know.'

'I'd no idea that such doctrinal differences were important to the Kiowa and Comanche,' remarked Talbot, 'I'd have thought that one type of Christian was much the same as another.'

'Not a bit of it,' laughed Father O'Grady. 'Why, my converts here are always at loggerheads with the 'Water God Men'. They have the notion that only us with our crosses and statues are the real thing. I dare say the Baptists feel the same way.'

'Talking of Indians, Father,' said Talbot, 'there's something I feel I should tip you the wink about, if I might put it so.'

'What might that be, Mr Rogers?'

'Perhaps we could take a turn outside, just the two of us. I'd as soon keep this as between the two of us.' Talbot turned to Melanie and said, 'Don't take this amiss, Miss Barker. It's just a boring piece of business I need to talk over.'

'Don't you mind me,' Melanie assured him. 'Long as I can just sit here with this jug of juice and another piece of that ham, I'm fine.'

'That's the girl!' said Talbot, giving her a bright smile.

Once the two men were outside in the afternoon sun, the priest said, 'Well then, out with it. What don't you want that child to know?'

'I don't want her to be scared. There's no more to the case than that.'

'She doesn't strike me as one who scares that easily.'

Talbot pulled out from his jacket the envelope that he had received from Carson before he had died. He showed it to Father O'Grady and said, 'I have here a message for the soldier in charge at Fort Williams. It gives warning that the Kiowa are about to rise. Some of the Comanche might join them. From all I know of the Comanche, that's likely to be the first day after the full moon, what some know as a 'Comanche Moon'.'

'It's the first I've heard of it. Are you sure your information is reliable?'

'The man who gave me this letter died a few minutes later. I can't see why he would have wished to mislead me with death standing at his very shoulder, waiting to claim him.'

Father O'Grady stopped walking and turned a troubled face to Talbot. 'If what you say is true, Mr Rogers, then I have to warn my parishioners. Many of them are Kiowa and they'll need to seek safety here.'

The natural respect which Talbot Rogers felt for a man of the cloth struggled briefly with the desire to save a fellow being from the consequences of his own folly. Common sense triumphed over social convention and he exclaimed irritably, 'Are you quite mad? The last thing you must do is let on to any of the Indians that you know about this. They'll cut your throat without thinking twice!'

'I think that you may safely leave me to judge for myself how trustworthy are those who attend my services — ' began the priest.

Talbot cut in at this point, unable to restrain himself. 'Begging your pardon, Father, but it's not just your hide I'm thinking of here. It's like to take me and that child at least another day or two to reach Fort Williams and I won't have you setting a match to the powder train while we're still on the road.'

Much as his men respected and feared him, it was clear that they were all a little shaken up and disturbed by the way in which their leader had so needlessly put all of their lives at hazard. Nobody felt like halting their headlong flight from the scene of the latest killing until they were a good three miles from where they had encountered the three lawmen. When at last they did so, Bob Easton, who had been with Hilton for longer than any of them, said, 'What in the hell were you thinking of? Why did you do it?'

'Why?' asked Tom Hilton. 'Why'd I do it? I'll tell you why. No man has ever pointed a gun in my face like that without reaping the consequence of it. Nobody. I wasn't aiming for that mouthy bastard to break the run of it.'

'Any of us could have been shot,' said Easton, 'it was mad, Tom. Why'n't you own it?'

There was a deadly silence and just

when it was looking as though Bob Easton might be about to go the way of all flesh, Hilton burst out laughing and said, 'Ah shit, you're right, Bob. It was badly done and just my stupid pride. There now, we ain't a goin' to fall out over it, surely?'

Easton smiled reluctantly and said, 'Hell, no. But Tom, we all count on you. It'd be the very devil if something befell you, so don't take so many risks, hey?'

The others began breathing again. You never really knew with this man. One moment, you could be laughing and chatting with him, nice as pie; the next, he'd taken mortal offence at a chance word. There wasn't one of the men riding with him who hadn't thought that Hilton had done something right stupid that day, but only Bob Easton had the balls to brace their leader about it.

'Now I been lessoned,' said Hilton, winking at Easton to show he was just joking, 'maybe we can plan our next move. I guess that you fellows want some o' the plunder from this war that those damned savages are about to start?'

The man they called Ben stirred at hearing the Indians described as 'savages', but he said nothing. Tom Hilton continued, 'They won't be after paper money, that I do know. Gold, weapons, livestock and I don't know what all else, but not bills. If we can hit any towns just after the Kiowa have finished with them, then there'll be rich pickings, you can depend upon it. I'm telling you, boys, the good times are comin'!'

7

Father O'Grady proved to be immune to reason and so Talbot thought it best if he and young Melanie set off on their way as soon as could be. He said to the priest, 'We're mighty obliged to you for the food, as well as the chance to rest. Good luck with your people, Father.'

'God bless you, Mr Rogers. I appreciate your concern.'

'It's your funeral. It's no affair of mine. I just hope to deliver this young lady safely to Fort Williams and then I'll be a free agent again.'

As the two of them walked away from the mission, leading their horse along, Melanie said in a wistful voice, 'Have I been a real nuisance to you?'

The girl's sad tone touched Talbot's heart and he said, 'Don't take on so. You mustn't set any mind to what I say, I'm old and crabby is all. I'm just not used to looking after somebody, there's no more to it than that.'

'I guess you wish I hadn't've come with you then.'

Talbot smiled, saying, 'No, I wouldn't say that. Truth to tell, you've cheered me up a little. It's not often that I spend any time with a young person. You do me good.'

Although he was lying and had indeed wished that he had not become burdened with the child, she took his words at face value and smiled happily.

It was coming on towards evening by now and time that they were thinking of where to spend the night. Talbot said, 'Have you ever slept outside? Tell me the truth now.'

Melanie shook her head. 'I always wanted to, but my ma said it wasn't fittin' for a girl to stay out of doors the whole night through.'

'Well then, it'll be a regular novelty for you and no mistake. You know, I suppose, that you're apt to get cold and damp?'

'I don't mind.'

The two of them found a little grove of stunted trees, some quarter mile from the road. It didn't suit Talbot's notions of concealment precisely but it was better than nothing. The nearest hills were a couple of miles distant and it was his hope to reach Fort Williams this side of Christmas. Taking four or five mile detours wasn't the best means of achieving that end.

'There's only an old blanket here at back o' the saddle,' said Talbot, 'you best have that.'

'What about you?'

'I'll just lean with my back against yon' tree. I'll do well enough, I slept like that a mort o' times. Try and get some rest now.'

The girl shivered and said, 'Can't we light a fire or nothing? There looks to be a lot of dead wood. I reckon you could get a blaze going in next to no time.'

'Happen I could,' replied Talbot dryly, 'but I don't aim to be adoin' so. Lord, after we been shot at twice in the last couple of days, you think I'm after advertising our position to the world? Don't think it for a moment. Just try and sleep now. With luck, we'll hit Fort Williams some time tomorrow afternoon, God willing.' He then went off to hobble the mare, so that she wouldn't take too much catching in the morning.

★　★　★

Now by all the laws of chance, Talbot Rogers's path should never again have crossed that of Tom Hilton and his boys. It was, after all, a wide land and no reason for one man to bump into another, unless that is, he was wishing to do so. After the narrow escape from the cavalry patrol at Greenhaven and the killing of the deputy marshal up in the hills, even Tom Hilton knew that it would be pushing his luck to stretching point and beyond, were he to carry on down the vengeance trail in search of the man who had killed his brother. Much as he desired to murder this assassin, Tom Hilton saw no present prospect of being able to easily lay hands upon the man and so postponed thoughts of revenge for the time being.

Like Talbot Rogers and Melanie Barker, the Hilton gang slept out that night. Had they but known it, they were only a few miles from the mission station where Talbot and his young charge had received assistance the previous day. They knew nothing of this, however. When they rose at first light and prepared to make their way in the general direction of Fort Williams, Ben sniffed the air delicately and said, 'There's been a house or something burned down in the night. Sombody killed, too.'

'How'd you know so?' enquired another member of the band.

The 'breed shrugged. 'I can smell it on the wind. You white folk aren't worth shit as trackers and such. Really, you can't smell burned man-flesh?'

Tom Hilton, who trusted Ben's instincts and knew that they weren't apt to lead him astray, said, 'Which way is this fire?'

'Right where we're heading, towards Fort Williams.'

'You think this rising has already begun?'

Ben shrugged and said, 'Those I spoke to were certain-sure as it was scheduled for another day or so. Who knows what might have chanced since then?'

Hilton stood thinking for a space and then said, 'Well then, we'll keep to the same track. Maybe we'll see what caused this. Either way, I want to be near Fort Williams when the fat gets in the fire. If we ain't careful, we's goin' to miss out on the richest pickings here.'

It was accordingly agreed that the party would proceed cautiously in the direction of what the 'breed said was a fire and then see what was what. Then they would try to hit Fort Williams just a few paces behind the Kiowa war parties. It was a hell of a risk, but these were men who had lived with danger for the whole of their adult lives. If things ran smoothly, they might pick up enough between them to give up the game altogether and maybe buy a homestead, share of a saloon or cat house; as their various inclinations directed.

★ ★ ★

'I'm aching all over and freezing cold,' said Melanie Barker, 'I surely could do with a hot breakfast.'

'You'll get nothing of the kind out here,' replied Talbot unsympathetically. 'Might I remind you that you begged me to bring you along on this trip? If you recollect correctly, you'll know as I advised against it from the start.'

This was unanswerable and the girl contorted her face in what is known in a pretty girl as 'making a moue' and in a plain one, 'pulling a face'. The only sustenance was the remains of the loaf from the previous day, washed down with draughts of cold water. While they broke their fast in this cheerless fashion, Talbot Rogers peered towards the horizon, back the way they had come from and said, 'I don't care for that plume of smoke. Unless I miss my guess, that's right where that mission station stands. Or stood, which is most likely. We need to move right fast, Miss Melanie.'

With the girl mounted up on the horse, and Talbot walking briskly by her side, they set off in the direction which he fervently hoped would soon bring them in sight of Fort Williams. As they went, Talbot Rogers cast occasional, anxious glances over his shoulder, where the faint and distant smudge of dark smoke could be seen trickling up to the clear blue sky. He'd warrant in a court of law that the mission station had been put to the torch and if that was so, then the odds were that his quest was in vain. By the time they reached Fort Williams, that too would most likely have been burned and sacked.

Talbot was sensitive enough not to wish to communicate any of his fears to the child riding at his side as he strode along, and he said brightly, 'Well, Miss, and how do you care for roughing it like a seasoned campaigner?'

'I don't like it at all,' she told him frankly, 'and if I never sleep out of doors again, that will be just fine for me. Say, we finished that bread. What'll we do for our midday meal?'

'Blessed if I know. Says in the Good Book that the Lord will provide.'

'Well,' she responded, tartly and impiously, 'I wish He'd get on and do it. My belly's already protesting.'

★　★　★

As Tom Hilton and the others were within a mile of the smouldering remains of the mission station, they noticed that another group of riders were also heading towards it, from the opposite direction. The two bands of horsemen were equidistant from their intended destination and although a good two miles separated them, Hilton could see that these others were riding in a neat and compact column. They were moreover clad in blue tunics.

'Ah hell,' muttered Hilton, 'that's the very Devil. I surely hope it ain't that same bunch we saw at Greenhaven. If so, we're apt to have some explaining to do.'

'We could cut and run,' suggested one of the men, 'Make for those hills over to the left.'

'I reckon as you must have dung for brains!' exclaimed Tom Hilton wrathfully. 'What ails you? We run now and those boys'll make sure we're up to no good. No, we got to front it out. I don't want them to get the idea as we're on the scout.'

'No,' said Ben, whether ironically or not, it was impossible to tell, 'that would never do!'

The two troops of riders, the bandits and the detachment of cavalry, arrived at the remains of the mission station more or less simultaneously. There was an uneasy pause, with both bands staring, at least to begin with, not at each other but at the grisly tableau in front of the smoking shell of the mission station. A black-robed figure was spread-eagled against the one remaining wall of the building; his arms impaled to the adobe by bayonets, in a grotesque parody of the crucifixion. The corpse bristled like a porcupine with arrows.

As the men gazed in horrified fascination at this ghastly sight, their nostrils were assailed by a sickening odour of charred meat, which put some of them in mind of a barbecue. There were no roast hogs in the case though, as the blackened body that lay across the threshold of the former chapel testified. The tang in the air was from what Ben the 'breed had earlier described correctly and succinctly as the 'smell of burned man-flesh'. Some of the cavalry troopers looked sick with the horror of the thing.

The first thing that Tom Hilton and his boys always asked themselves in an awkward situation was, can we shoot our way free of this? In the present case, it would have been little short of madness even to consider such a notion. There were thirty riders in the cavalry troop and one look at them indicated at once that these were men on active service. They were heavily armed and seemingly well-prepared for any eventuality. Not only that, but having absorbed the dreadful scene in front of them, most of them were now gazing suspiciously at Hilton and the others, perhaps trying to gauge if these men had had any part in the butchery of the men at the mission station.

The major in command of the troop broke the tense silence by asking, 'Who might you boys be and what are you doing hereabouts?'

This was by way of being a delicate subject and for a moment, Tom Hilton was stumped and said nothing. The others did not wish to appear to be pushing themselves forward, with all the attendant risk of bringing down their leader's wrath upon their heads at some later time, and so none of them spoke. When the lack of response was becoming notable and likely to provoke suspicion in the officer who had asked the question, a man called Steve Coulton said impulsively, 'We's pilgrims.'

'Pilgrims?' asked the major. 'That's blazing strange to hear. What kind of pilgrimage are you on? Out with it quick, now. We have urgent matters to attend to.'

Coulton, who was in fact a lapsed Catholic, said, 'We're agoin' to the shrine of Our Lady, away over by El Paso.'

'I heard of it. You boys don't look like what I'd describe as the religious sort, though. You best not be making game of me. Any o' you know aught of this business?'

'The killing and such, you mean? No, I am truly grieved to see a man of the cloth slain. When you men arrived, I was about to suggest to my fellow travellers as it might be fittin' to offer up a prayer for the repose of this man's soul.'

For a second or two, the cavalry officer stared in frank disbelief at Steve Coulton, before saying brusquely, 'Well then, get on with it. Time's pressing.'

Taking their lead from Coulton, Tom Hilton and the other seven men dismounted and followed Steve over to the crucified priest. It was like some dreadful game of charades, because if the cavalry realized that they were being tricked, then there was a very real chance that they would assume that the supposed pilgrims and penitents who had attempted to pull the wool over their eyes were really connected in some way with the sacking of the mission station. At best, they would be taken prisoner; at worst, perhaps shot out of hand. The soldiers looked as though they were primed and ready for any kind of action.

Steve Coulton removed his hat and the other men, who had evidently decided that the safest course of action was simply to imitate Coulton in every way, did the same.

'Dear Lord,' said Coulton huskily, 'we ask you to take to your bosom this faithful servant of your'n, who's met a fearful end. We ask it in thy name. Amen.'

Tom Hilton and the other seven men piously echoed Coulton, chorusing his 'amen'.

'Now I'll just say a couple o' prayers,' announced Coulton, getting into the swing of his burlesque, 'startin' with an Ave and then saying a Paternoster.'

Coulton's early raising at a Jesuit school stood him in good stead, as he rattled off the Lord's Prayer and Hail Mary in tolerably good Latin. At the end of each prayer, he paused, so that all of them pronounced the 'amen' together.

As they turned back to the major, it was clear to every one of them, by the look on his face, that he was not wholly satisfied by this outward display of piety. However, he had other and more important matters to attend to, chiefly the suppression of what was rapidly taking on the appearance of a general uprising by all the Indians in this part of the country. There was no time even to investigate the attack on this isolated mission, and he had already wasted time here. The murders here told Major Carter all that he needed to know about the rumours that had reached Fort Williams about the restless nature of the local tribes. It was imperative now that he both continued with his own mission and also sent word back to his base to warn them to assume a posture of war.

The major surveyed the group of 'pilgrims' for a space, running his eyes over each of them in turn. He could hardly burden himself with nine prisoners at this juncture; nor did he feel able to deal with these villainous-looking individuals by executing them without a trial. After a few moments, he came up with what seemed to him to be an ideal solution to his dilemma, one which would shift the onus for figuring out what kind of wrongdoing, if any, these men were about.

Major Carter announced, 'You men may be heading over to El Paso for some reason. But it would be madness for you to ride through the wild country right now. 'Case you've not heard, the Kiowa are rising. If I suspected for a second that you were running guns to the redskins or aught of the sort, I tell you now: it be all up with you.' He paused, to allow the full import of his words to sink in. Then he continued, 'Howsoever, I don't see my way to suspicion you all on the evidence as it stands. Here's what we'll do, for your safety as well as mine. I have to send a messenger straight back to Fort Williams and tell of what I have found here this day. They need to be warned. So I'll send a rider back along of you boys. There's safety in numbers and then when you get to the fort . . . well, then we'll see what they make there of this 'pilgrimage' of yours.'

For all that he was a battle-hardened veteran of the Indian Wars, there was a touching naïvety about the cavalry major which rejoiced the hearts of Tom Hilton and the others. It was as plain as a pikestaff that the thought did not for a moment cross the mind of this decent man that any white man, however depraved, would dream of raising his hand against a trooper of the United States Cavalry. The Hilton gang could scarcely believe their luck.

'That's right good of you, sir,' said Tom Hilton, his voice quivering with genuine and unfeigned gratitude. He truly could not believe that Coulton had fooled the major so easily. 'Me and the others will be glad of the company and reassured by having one of your men riding along of us.'

'Well, mind I don't have cause to repent of the action. Make certain-sure that you repay my trust.'

So it was that instead of being taken off in irons or shot, both of which had seemed realistic prospects a half hour earlier, the nine bandits found themselves riding hard in the direction in which they wished to go, accompanied by a pleasant and good-natured youngster of nineteen, with no more guile about him than a babe in arms. Matters could hardly have turned out better and later that day, some of them took to joshing Steve Coulton that those prayers he spoke must have been mighty powerful and that maybe they should all take up as Catholics, if that's what their petitions to the Almighty were able to accomplish.

★   ★   ★

The fort hove into view sooner than Talbot Rogers had expected. Their way had led him and Melanie to a craggy range of hills, the slopes of which were riven with chasms and scattered with boulders. The track wended its way through a miniature canyon, until the two of them emerged into the open, with a wide plain stretched out before them. There in the distance stood an army fort, its towering walls constructed of creosoted wood. Next to it, they could just make out two small settlements which had grown up in the lea of the military base. On one side was a straggling line of log cabins and other little buildings; on the other, what looked to be an Indian village made up of tepees. Talbot rubbed his chin meditatively and said, 'I wonder what they're about, letting the Indians camp so close to the fort.'

'Ain't it usual to do so?'

'It's not common. I seen it before, up at Fort Laramie, in Wyoming. Didn't much care for the arrangement up there, neither.'

The girl opened her mouth to make some reply, but Talbot held up his hand, saying, 'Hush up. I can hear something.' He listened intently for a moment and then said, 'There's a bunch o' riders headed this way. Happen we'd do well to get off the road. Move quickly now. Hop down from that horse.'

The two of them and the horse moved into a rocky defile which led into some chasm within the cliffs which reared up behind them. By this time, even Melanie could hear the thunder of hoofs and was struck with a sudden terror, recollecting the bloody deaths that she had witnessed over the last few days. She leaned against Talbot Rogers for comfort and assurance. He put his arm gently around her shoulders and murmured, 'There, there. Like as not, it's nothing to be affeared of.'

★　★　★

The young trooper whose job it was to accompany them to Fort Williams, was the most trusting of individuals and all of them could sense at once that he did not entertain the least apprehension about the men riding along with him.

He gossiped about the difficulties of army life, the scandalous behaviour of the officers at the fort, his home in Kansas and 101 other things. Tom Hilton thought that it was as good as a play to hear the boy chatter on in this way; he was that fresh and innocent. Hilton was by no means a sensitive or sentimental man, but even he felt that it was a pity that the kid would have to die.

8

When Hilton and his men had been riding for a half hour or so and it was certain that they were well clear of the troop of cavalry whom they had encountered at the mission station, Hilton cried out, 'Whoa, rein in there!'

The eight men of his band all obeyed this command immediately. The young trooper took a little longer; trotting forward for a few seconds, until he found that the others had all halted. He wheeled his horse round and went back, saying, 'Hey, you fellows! What's to do?'

Hilton addressed the youngster in a regretful, almost fatherly tone of voice. He said, 'What it is, young man, is that it don't precisely accord with our plans to have that fort alerted of the hazard it's facing. Queers our pitch, so to speak.'

'I don't rightly understand you,'

began the boy, as one of Hilton's men moved up behind him and plucked the trooper's carbine from where it nestled in its scabbard. At this action, the young man whirled round angrily and then saw that all the men were looking at him soberly. It was at this point that he realized that the remaining seconds of his life were slipping inexorably away. He was a game one though, and didn't show the slightest fear, merely observing contemptuously, 'Why, you bunch of skunks! You'd murder me to further some game of your own? Well then . . .'
He was speaking only to hold their attention and without any warning, reached down and tried to extricate his pistol from its holster. Unfortunately, he was wearing not some gunslinger's rig, but a stiff, leather holster which had a flap buttoned over the hilt of the pistol to prevent it falling out while a man was on horseback. The boy had only managed to undo the button, when Tom Hilton's ball took him in the chest and he toppled sideways from the

saddle. His horse jittered sideways and was still. By the time the echo of the shot had died down, it was all over with the young soldier.

'Didn't he die well, boys?' said Hilton. There was a chorus of assent, with people making remarks such as, 'He weren't a bit afraid!' and 'He was a game one, all right!' If there was one thing which these men respected, it was fearlessness in the face of death and from their point of view, though exceedingly young, the trooper had shown himself to be a real man.

'Still and all,' said Tom Hilton, after a few seconds pause in appreciation of the man whose life he had so casually snuffed out, 'this ain't business. Strikes me as things are moving pretty damned fast and if we don't make tracks to Fort Williams this very minute, we're like to lose out on whatever pickings are to be had from this here rising.' He shouted, 'Yah!' and spurred on his horse. The others rode after him.

As the riders swept past their hiding place, Talbot Rogers risked a peek over the top of a boulder, at their retreating backs. There was nothing remarkable about the appearance of this body of men, and he would have been wholly unable to explain why he felt so, but Talbot knew, deep in his bones, that these men meant mischief and were up to no good. It was that lawman's sixth sense, which warned him to stay concealed and wait until the men were well away. It was just as well, because as they rode away, the position of the horsemen altered slightly and he caught a brief glimpse of crimson at the neck of one of the men. It would have been the damnedest coincidence for Talbot to spot two such men in the area in the space of a day or two. He stared thoughtfully after the retreating riders and thought to himself, Unless I miss my guess, there goes one of them as killed young Melanie's pa.

Melanie said, 'Who are they? Anybody you know?'

'I couldn't say. Something's amiss, though.'

'How so?'

'Can't put it into words, Miss Melanie, but those boys are heading in the same direction as us and I wish that they weren't. Well, let be what will. We'd best be setting off towards the fort. But before we go, I want an assurance from you.'

'What is it? Have I done something wrong?'

Talbot smiled and said, 'Don't fret, you been a good girl so far. No, I just want you to promise me that you do exactly as I bid you, without any debate. Once we're in sight of Fort Williams, I mean.'

'Do you expect trouble?'

'I always expect trouble. It's by way of being an old habit o' mine. In the present case, though, I think as I'm entirely justified in it. Lord knows why, but I seem to have taken responsibility for you, child. That being so, I need you to do just as you're told. At once, mind.'

The girl looked crestfallen and forlorn, saying sadly, 'I been a trial to you and no mistake.'

'Nothing of the sort. You've acted on me like a tonic and made the journey more pleasant.'

Her face brightened at once and she said, 'Truly?'

'Yes, truly. But we spent enough time chattering here like old women. We needs must move on as fast as we can now. There's something afoot as I don't care for, though I can't quite make out what it might be.'

★ ★ ★

The little town which had sprung up in the shelter of Fort Williams contained no more than a hundred souls. In general, they provided services for the soldiers stationed at the fort, things that they would otherwise have been compelled to forego. There was a liquor store, which doubled as a cantina in the evenings, a general store and also a cathouse, perhaps the smallest in the whole country. A log cabin, divided by hanging blankets, gave the facility for three men at a

156

time to satisfy their desires with three farm girls who had been lured out into Texas on the promise of becoming actresses and dancers in musical theatres.

The Indian settlement, which lay on the other side of the fort, provided broadly similar services and goods and the two villages vied constantly for the soldiers' business. The Indians, Kiowa in the main, also ran a miniscule cathouse on an even more modest scale than that operated by the white men on the other side of the fort.

Relations between the fort and the various civilians who lived around it were cordial. Indeed, the main gate to the fort was only locked at night. At other times, traders, whores, peddlers, scouts and many other types and conditions of men and women simply walked freely in and out of the place. It was this which the men organizing the uprising hoped to take advantage of. For in addition to the complement of cavalry which manned the base, there was an arsenal which contained many hundreds of muskets and a vast store of powder and shot for the same. The government in Washington, even at this time, two years before the beginning of the great War Between the States, wished to keep plentiful supplies of weaponry scattered about the country. This was so that if ever the calls for states' rights became too strident and threatened to spill over into armed confrontation, the federal government would have enough guns to distribute to men of good will; those, in other words, who would side with Washington in any dispute with the South.

They say that familiarity breeds contempt and complacency. This was without the shadow of a doubt the case at Fort Williams. So used were those stationed at the base to seeing both white people and Indians wandering around, that they hardly gave a thought anymore to the security of the rifles with which they had been entrusted. After all, the country was presently at peace and doubtless they would be given good notice if that were about to change.

The day before Tom Hilton and his men rode up to Fort Williams, the Officer Commanding had received word that there were stirrings of discontent among the local tribes. He didn't set much store by this; there were always rumours of some sort floating around, but as a precaution he had despatched a patrol to scout about and see what they might uncover. It was this group which the Hilton gang had encountered at the burned out mission station. As a further measure, Colonel Russell forbade any Indians to enter the fort, although white folk were still permitted to come and go, providing they left their guns at the gate. Sentries enforced this new rule, which nobody expected to last for long.

When Hilton and his men rode up to the fort, they half hoped to find it already ransacked and abandoned, allowing them to help themselves to whatever the Kiowa had not thought worth taking. However, one glance told them that it must be business as usual there.

'I don't see sign of any massacres or

nothing,' remarked Ben. 'Looks as quiet as quiet can be, you ask me.'

'Thinkin' the same thing myself,' replied Hilton moodily. 'Were it not for that mission station and the cavalry back there, I might think we been sold a cat in a sack over this.'

The nine men dismounted, tethering their horses to hitching posts outside the general store. Hilton said, 'What say we take a turn in this famous fort and see what we might see?'

There were nods and grunts at this. Hilton continued, 'Let's not all march in like we're bandits or something. We'll drift in in twos and threes, so nobody marks us.'

It is said that man proposes, but God disposes and so it proved that day. Tom Hilton invited the 'breed to enter the fort in his company, but they were peremptorily stopped at the gate by two sentries who asked Ben, 'Where d'you think you're agoin'?'

'Why, just to do a little business in this fort o' yours. What's the difficulty?'

'Well now, we ain't welcoming Redskins into our place just now, so there's an end to it.'

The 'breed stood there, baffled and furious. At last, he said, 'I ain't an Indian.'

'Well, you surely ain't a white man. Now get on out of here.' The guard turned to Hilton, saying, 'You can enter, but you've to leave your gun here. You can have it again when you leave.'

Tom Hilton turned to Ben and said mildly, 'You cut along back to your friends, now. I'll catch up with you later.'

It did not escape Hilton's notice that despite confiscating the piston he carried in a holster at his hip, no attempt was made to search him for arms. This struck him as peculiarly inept and suggested that it would probably be possible to smuggle a gun into the fort, were one determined to do so. This might be useful to know.

★ ★ ★

Talbot and Melanie reached Fort Williams while Tom Hilton and a few of his men were wandering around inside the army base, working out what it would take for a determined band of men to seize the arsenal there.

'I'm awful thirsty,' exclaimed Melanie, 'do you think we can get some soda or something?'

Talbot looked at the girl fondly and said, 'We can try. More to the point, we can find the relatives that your dead pa, God rest him, was bringing you to visit.' While he spoke, Talbot caught sight of a group of men who were standing down the single street of the village a little way and realized that these were the very men who he had seen gallop past earlier that day. Watching them covertly, he was confirmed in his impression that here were no innocent travellers, but rather a bunch of fellows up to some villainy or other. He said to Melanie, 'I'm telling you, honey, the sooner I can hand you on to your folks, the better I shall be. Not 'cause I don't take to your company, but on account of there's trouble brewing and I don't want you standing at my side when the lightning strikes.'

'Well, the only thing is, I don't rightly know at all who these kin of mine are.'

'You must have a name or something, surely?'

The girl shook her head and replied, 'Nothing o' the kind. My pa, he just said as he'd settle everything once we reached Fort Williams. That's all I know on it.'

A sudden and horrifying thought struck Talbot and he said, 'It was Fort Williams that your pa was heading for, wasn't it?'

Melanie puckered up her forehead with deep thought and eventually said, 'I don't know that it was, you know. We were surely heading for the fort, but now you mention it, I've a notion that these kin of his lived beyond here.'

Talbot Rogers cursed himself for a fool. Now that he thought back, he realized with a sinking heart that the name

Fort Williams had never actually been mentioned by the girl as her final destination. He'd merely jumped to a hasty conclusion. He said, 'Let's try and get you something to drink, while we figure out what's what. First, I must make provisions for this beast.'

★ ★ ★

There were so many people milling about in the fort that Hilton and the two men at his side didn't stand out at all. It wasn't hard to tell which building was the arsenal. Most of the fort was constructed of hewn logs, liberally coated with creosote, but bang in the centre of the compound stood a stone-built block-house, with barred windows and a guard standing sentry-go at the door.

'That's the arsenal, for a bet!' said Tom Hilton. 'Can't see anybody breaking in there in a hurry.' As they strolled about the fort, trying to look as though they were on their way to conduct some important business, perhaps with some of the officers at the base, Hilton began to think it increasingly likely that he'd led the men on a snipe hunt. It all looked as calm and peaceful as could be and if the Kiowa started anything, it looked to him as though there would be plenty of soldiers to stop them. Things began looking up, though, when they retrieved their weapons from the sentries and went back outside to rejoin the others.

It was obvious that the 'breed had good news, for he could scarcely keep from smiling.

'Well,' said Hilton, 'You look like the cat as got the cream and no mistake. Out with it, what you heard?'

'I dropped by that village over yonder. Met a fellow I knew a while back. There's trouble in the wind all right, but we might need to get more involved.'

'How's that?'

'This is the way of it. Tonight, Kiowa were to enter the fort in ones and twos and then kill enough of the soldiers to allow a whole bunch of their men to enter and seize the arsenal. There's a heap of 'em waiting up in the hills this minute. Howsoever, word got out and now the soldiers won't allow any Indians at all in, like we saw. Searching all the white folk going in as well.'

'You seem full of all the news,' grunted Hilton, concealing his delight. 'What's more?'

'This. If we can somehow open up that fort tonight, then the Kiowa'll let us help ourselves to all the bills in the place. It'll come to a tidy sum and we're sure to pick up other cash if the thing spreads across Texas. I'm tellin' you, this could be the making of us.'

Tom Hilton suddenly grinned; a rare occurrence for him. He said, 'I do declare, you're like as not right about that. You sure you can trust these people?'

The 'breed shrugged. 'Much as you can trust anybody, I guess.'

'Then I guess we're in business,' said Hilton. 'Let's go aways from anybody and talk over our plans. You can arrange for word to reach the Kiowa up in the hills?'

'Surely,' said Ben, 'long as we don't leave it too late.'

★ ★ ★

Asking in the stores failed to unearth anybody who would own any connection or kinship with Melanie's deceased father, which, thought Talbot Rogers privately, was a damned nuisance. Still, there it was. He was keenly aware that he should not have delayed handing over the letter that the dying man had entrusted to him to the senior officer at the fort. There was nothing for it, but to keep the child alongside him, until it was convenient to enquire more deeply into the matter. Talbot felt that he could hardly, with a clear conscience, abandon the girl in a rough place such as this and leave her to fend for her own self.

'Looks like you and me, young

Melanie,' he told her, 'are to remain in each other's company for a little while longer. It can't be helped.'

'Oh, I don't mind a bit. Am I to stay in a real bed tonight? I'm already wore out.'

Despite his irritation at finding that he was to continue looking after her, Talbot Rogers could not help smiling. He had had so little to do with young people in recent years, that the child's animal vitality and good spirits were a novelty of which he had not yet tired. He said, 'God willing, the two of us will be able to rest here tonight. I saw some establishment akin to a commercial hotel, although the Lord only knows what the beds will be like in a backward little place like this. But yes, I reckon at the least I may engage to find you a bed. First, we have to visit that fort. I have business there which won't wait.'

The fact that he was relieved of his pistol before being permitted to enter the fort, reassured Talbot that some precautions at least were being observed.

He overheard two men talking and gathered that Indians were completely forbidden from coming in and that this was by way of being a recent development. This too indicated that perhaps the news he bore would not come altogether as a surprise to those in charge of Fort Williams. He had asked the trooper who had taken his gun, where he might find the commanding officer and been directed to the adjutant's office. That gentleman was by no means inclined to cooperate, asking Talbot bluntly what business he had with the colonel.

'It's a confidential matter . . . ' began Talbot, only to have the other man cut in with the greatest irascibility.

'Yes, I'll be bound it is. Just tell me what you are selling and I'll pass the news on to Colonel Russell. 'Less'n it's snake oil for his rheumatics, in which case I can tell you now, it won't answer.'

'I have an urgent communication for the Colonel. It was entrusted to me by a dying man and relates to an Indian rising. There, does that alter the case?'

Melanie Barker, irrepressible as always, interrupted at this point to ask Talbot, 'Say, was that the fellow with the peg-leg, as was shot? I wondered what you were about with him.'

The adjutant, a young captain, said, 'Without knowing more of the matter, there's little I can do. Who was this man? Him that died, I mean.'

'His name was Carson.'

'Not Tobias Carson?'

'That's more than I can tell you. I never learned his given name, on account of he died not five minutes after first I spoke to him. All I know is that he worked for the Indian Bureau.'

The young officer rubbed his chin thoughtfully, saying, 'This casts another light, I do confess. This communication, was it verbal or written?'

'It's a letter.'

'You have it here, with you now? I ask, because Colonel Russell left here an hour since.'

Talbot hesitated for a moment, weighing the business up. He had sworn to the man from the Indian Bureau that he would only deliver the letter to the officer commanding Fort Williams in person. It would be a fearful thing to break an oath made under such circumstances. It looked, though, as if affairs were moving towards some kind of climax; if he was any judge of such things.

Something of what was going through Talbot Rogers's mind must have shown on his face, for the adjutant said, 'If this has any bearing upon the intentions of the Kiowa nation, then I beg that you will share your information this minute, sir. We know here about Mr Carson and when he left, the Colonel was hoping to receive some word from him. I cannot tell you how desperately urgent this is.'

'I reckon,' said Talbot slowly, 'that in a fix like this, a man has to trust his instincts. If you give me your word that your commanding officer is not present, nor like to be this day, then I guess I'll leave this here letter in your hands and consider that I have done my best.' He reached into his jacket and withdrew the long, white envelope; reaching across the desk to hand it to the captain.

9

Tom Hilton was not in general overly fond of half-breeds, but he had ridden with Ben long enough to know that whatever else he might be, the 'breed was a trustworthy and loyal comrade. If he said that the Kiowa would allow Hilton and his men to loot whatever the Indians themselves had no use for, then that was the way of it. Of course, it was still a damned risky undertaking and there was always the possibility of catching a stray bullet or arrow when the fighting began, to say nothing of the Kiowa suddenly changing their minds and killing them as well as the soldiers in the fort, but then that was no more than the usual hazard constantly present for all those men who lived, as the Hilton gang did, on the wrong side of the law. The rewards, when they came, could be enormous but so too were the risks.

The arsenal inside the fort was the key to everything. The government in Washington had for some months been stockpiling weaponry at bases such as this in the southern states. In later years, the reason for such movements of arms would appear quite obvious. It would be another eighteen months before the Confederates shelled the Yankees out of Fort Sumter, signalling the beginning of the War Between the States, but already large quantities of rifles, powder and shot were being sent south and stored at places like Fort Williams. The government was already preparing for possible attempts at succession by states such as Texas and Georgia, and wished to be able to arm those who supported the federal government at a moment's notice.

If the Kiowa were to have any chance at all in their rising, then it was imperative that they were well armed, which was not at all the current situation. True, some of them had rifles and pistols, but not all of them by any means. If the contents of the arsenal could somehow be distributed though, there would be enough to provide muskets and ammunition for over 3,000 warriors. By the time military forces could be transferred from the north to deal with such an insurrection, a large swathe of the southern United States might have fallen into Indian hands. This at least was how some viewed the case.

Ben had been back to the little village of tepees and when he rejoined the others, he told them that the forces mustering in the hills were all but out of provisions and that it was vital that they swept down upon Fort Williams without any further delay. Under present circumstances, with the army on the alert, then such an attack would be hopeless. Their only chance lay in riding straight into the fort and taking the forces there by complete surprise. As he explained to the others, 'They close up the gate to that place and start firing down from the ramparts, our boys won't have a chance. It'll be a massacre.'

'Our boys?' asked Tom Hilton, an ironic smile on his lips, 'I'm hopeful that you're not forgetting which side you're on here, Ben my boy.'

For a moment, the 'breed looked discomforted, but he went on to say, 'Anywise, once those gates is shut and the troopers on alert, there ain't a cat in hell's chance o' the Kiowa taking the arsenal. Not to mention where what they call the element of surprise is gone. Every base in Texas'll be on a war footing in next to no time.'

'Seems to me you thought that thing through right well,' said Hilton approvingly. 'I read it the same way. I surely hate to give up on this though and so here's what I come up with. We can lend a hand to those fellows up in the hills and kind of even up the odds a little.'

Seeing the puzzled looks on the faces of the eight men listening to him, Tom Hilton chuckled and exclaimed jovially,

'Ain't you men learned to trust me by now? Here's what I say.'

★ ★ ★

The adjutant read through the letter slowly and carefully. Having done so, he looked up and said, 'I don't see that this tells us much more than is already known. There's trouble among the Kiowa and we're already tackling it. There's no more to it than that.'

'Fellow I spoke to thought it was life and death.'

'How did he die? Was it Indians?'

'No, road agents. It was a stupid business. When is your Colonel expected back?'

'That's a military question. It needn't concern any civilian. I will pass this letter on to my commanding officer when he returns, but now I must bid you good day. I have many duties and responsibilities to tend to in his absence, as I am sure you will apprehend.'

After the two of them had been practically turfed out of the adjutant's office, Talbot muttered to his young companion, 'Pompous young fool. I know his sort. So puffed up with his own importance that he's lost sight of what he should be doing.'

Melanie was slightly shocked to hear Mr Rogers speaking with such vehemence and she said, 'Are you really mad at him?'

He collected himself and said, 'Well, he's a fool and I should just leave him to it. I can't, though, for if that fort falls, then I see no prospect of returning you safely to your family. The whole state'll be in an uproar. No, I guess I'll have to do something about it.'

'What will you do?'

'I haven't precisely decided yet. I wish there were somewhere I could leave you where you'd be safe.'

Although she didn't wish to leave his side, Melanie Barker thought that she should try and be helpful, so she said, 'Don't worry about me, Mr Rogers. I can just linger around the town here. I'll be fine.'

'Nothing of the sort. First off, it's as rough as all get out and push here, and secondly, it's outside the walls of the fort. Any fighting and all those in this settlement will be the first to die.'

For all that she liked to give the impression of being a harum scarum, daredevil sort of girl, until a week ago Melanie had never encountered any worse danger in her life than an angry mother and a strict schoolteacher. Having witnessed in the last few days a number of bloody deaths, including that of her own father, and hearing now of the idea of everybody in a town being massacred was all suddenly too much for her and with no warning at all, she burst into tears.

Talbot had no idea at all how to deal with a young girl who was giving vent to fear in this way, sobbing convulsively and with tears streaming down her face. He did the only thing he could think of and put his arms around her, murmuring, 'There, there,' over and over. It seemed to do the trick, for after a space her crying subsided and she said, 'Oh, I could die of shame! You must think me a real cry baby.'

He answered truthfully, 'I thought it the most natural thing in the world, given how things stand for you right now.'

According to Ben the 'breed, there were perhaps 500 Kiowa warriors up in the hills, waiting to descend upon Fort Williams and seize the arsenal. If and when that end was accomplished, then Kiowa from across that part of Texas would converge on the fort and be issued with weapons. There were in the fort, as far as Hilton and his boys had been able to gauge, maybe 150 troopers. Another hundred or so had left earlier that day, which was handy.

'I calculate though, as we can give those Indians an edge,' said Tom Hilton, when he reasoned the matter out to his men. 'If those cavalry boys are organized in battle formation and a straight fight's made of it, why then, it may be all over in a minute or two.'

'So we might as well just leave it and go across the border with those bearer bonds,' said one man incautiously, 'You're saying it's no go.'

'You shut up and listen for a bit,' said Hilton sharply, 'and I'll tell you what's what. If there's chaos and everybody jumbled up together, with no clear line of fire, then it'll be hand to hand fighting. Then numbers will count and those friends of Ben here, will stand to come out on top. Specially if we can reduce the tally of soldiers by a little and get them running round like headless chickens into the bargain.'

The nine of them were seated on the ground, far enough away from both the fort and the little town that nobody was apt to be able to eavesdrop on them. Hilton knew that he had their attention and that if he showed them a plan that wasn't likely to result in their deaths, then they would follow him. He said, 'There's a mess hall in that fort, seats fifty men or so at a time. If all the men setting down there were to be killed, that would reduce the strength holding the fort to just a hundred. Those Kiowa would outnumber 'em five to one in hand to hand battle.'

There were uneasy stirrings at what sounded to the others awfully like starting a war with the United States Cavalry; a prospect relished by nobody. Hilton laughed a little contemptuously. 'Ain't I always led you boys to rich pickings? You scared to follow me now, is that it?'

'There's no call to speak o' being scared,' growled one man. 'I don't reckon anybody ever dared hint of such a thing to me in the whole course o' my life. Sounds like you want to take on 150 soldiers. That's just plumb crazy. Tell us plainly what you purpose.'

There was an uneasy silence and the others watched Tom Hilton to see how he would take this. He said, 'It's a fair question, I will allow. Here's the way of it. We get together a few pounds of fine-grain powder and a gallon or two of lamp oil. Then I'll engage to take out a third of the men at that fort and let the Kiowa ride in and deal with the rest.'

★   ★   ★

Two powerful impulses contended for mastery within Talbot Rogers's breast. One was to just dig up and leave, letting the US Cavalry deal with things as seemed best to them, without any help or assistance from him. This was a tempting notion, but Talbot knew that it wouldn't answer. As a former member of the armed forces, with many years service behind him, he could no more abandon this dangerous situation than fly to the moon. A complicating factor was that having decided that he was not currently able to surrender the care of the girl he was looking after to anybody else, he would be encumbered with her while trying to prevent what could amount to the onset of a war. Little wonder then that he muttered under his breath, 'This is the hell of a thing!'

Melanie Barker did not quite hear what had been said and so asked, 'Were you speaking to me, Mr Rogers?'

'No, child, don't you fret. It seems that our paths are likely to continue side by side for a spell and so I must extract a solemn assurance from you that you will do just exactly as I tell you for the next few hours. Will you promise me that?'

'Of course I will, sir. I'm right grateful for the help you've given me so far.'

'Good girl. Now I just want that you should wait here for five minutes, without talking to anybody or getting yourself into mischief. Reckon you can manage that?'

'Surely I can. I ain't a kid, you know!'

Talbot Rogers tucked his pistol in the back of his pants and then checked that his jacket concealed it from view. As good fortune would have it, the sentries at the gate of Fort Williams were being changed at that very moment, which was a relief to Talbot. It would have been a little awkward to try this trick on the same fellow who had already seen him go into the fort already, not fifteen minutes since.

One of the troopers standing sentry-go at the gate asked, as Talbot made to enter, 'Wait up, fellow. You carrying?'

Talbot flipped open his jacket to show that he wasn't wearing a gun-belt and enquired ironically, 'You want that I should empty my pockets, case I got a Derringer or something?'

The soldier laughed and said cheerfully, 'No, you don't look much like a killer. Go on, you can pass through.'

Talbot Rogers was not in general given to bad language, but once he had passed the sentry and entered the fort, he muttered under his breath the strongest expression he had used since leaving the army years ago. As he had suspected, it had been simplicity itself to carry two pistols into Fort Williams. In addition to the pistol he had tucked into the back of his pants, he also had the little muff pistol in his jacket pocket. For all their supposed precautions, the place was wide open to attack.

★ ★ ★

The plan that Hilton had devised would need split-second timing to come off, not to mention where it relied upon the good will and co-operation of a bunch of bloodthirsty savages. Such were the potential rewards, sufficient perhaps to enable every one of the gang to retire comfortably for the rest of their natural lives, that it seemed to them all an entirely reasonable gamble. They would infiltrate the fort in ones and twos, smuggling in powder and carrying openly kegs of lamp oil. With these materials, they would create such mayhem and bloodshed, that the whole fort would be in an uproar, with the troopers running round like headless chickens. At which point, they would deal with the sentries and open the way for the Kiowa to ride in and massacre the men stationed at Fort Williams. As long as the 'breed was playing straight and had actually struck a firm agreement with the warriors up in the hills and everybody knew how matters stood, then it might just work out all right.

As is so often the case with affairs of that sort though, the slightest little hitch would be quite sufficient to screw up the whole show. In this case, the factor that Hilton and his men, as well as the Kiowa, were overlooking was an insignificant-looking and colourless fellow who you wouldn't notice in a crowd. Just one man who knew the difference between right and wrong and was not about to back away from evil-doing when he saw it.

* * *

Just as Talbot Rogers had an instinct which enabled him to spot men like Carson from the Indian Bureau, those on the side of law and order, so too was he able to identify those on the other side of the street: bad men and those who kept company with them. It was as he was walking towards the wide open gate of the fort, in order to leave the place, that Talbot caught sight of three men walking slowly across the dusty parade ground which formed the heart of Fort Williams. Without a shadow of a doubt, Talbot Rogers knew that these men were up to no good. He speeded up a little and headed after them. Then when he was barely six feet behind them, and they altogether unaware of the fact that he was approaching, Talbot stumbled and made as though to fall to the ground. He put out a hand to save himself, almost knocking over one of the men as he steadied himself by touching the fellow's back.

Tom Hilton whirled round and exclaimed angrily, 'Mind what you're about, you clumsy old bastard! What d'you mean by it, touching me in such a way?'

'I beg pardon, I'm sure,' replied Talbot meekly, 'I lost my footing. I ain't as young as once I was and that's the fact of the matter.'

The two men stared into each other's eyes and for a moment, Hilton was oddly disconcerted. He shivered, as though a goose had walked over his grave. He looked harder at the apologetic little man standing before him and decided that he wasn't worth the bother of picking a fight with. Besides which, he had other fish to fry that day. Hilton limited himself to observing, 'Well, I say again, you're a clumsy bastard.'

'It may be so,' conceded Talbot mildly. 'In which case, I must once again apologize for being barging into you so.'

Hilton looked into the other's eyes, a slightly puzzled look upon his sharp features. The man whom he was insulting could scarcely have been more humble and self-effacing, yet there was something about the situation which did not somehow ring true. Then he realized that the sun was slowly sinking towards the western horizon and that there were plans to be made. He turned away abruptly and stalked off with his two companions.

As for Talbot Rogers, he was now completely satisfied in his own mind that the man he had allowed to abuse him was mixed up in some funny business. It wasn't just the sight of that red silk bandana around the fellow's throat which had confirmed him in this view. That had told him that here was one of those who had fired on them at Greenhaven, nothing more. More than that though, he was pretty sure that somehow these three men were mixed up with the Kiowa affair. It would be the hell of a coincidence if there were two plots involving the fort, both running parallel to each other, which meant that the three men who were walking away from him were almost certainly associated in some way with the projected Indian rising. Talbot wasn't a great believer in coincidence and so until further evidence turned up, he was compelled to assume that the

Kiowa and those three men had some common purpose linking them together.

Faking that false step and clutching at one of the men's back had been the perfect way of discovering if, like him, they were carrying concealed weapons into the fort. Putting all the pieces of the puzzle together told Talbot that something dangerous was afoot. He wouldn't have been able to take oath and swear to it in a court of law, but to his own satisfaction, he had established that something was about to happen in or around Fort Williams and since the army unit here didn't seem up to the job, he supposed that it would fall to him to deal with it.

* * *

Hilton said, 'If what Ben says is on the money, then if we set the match to the powder train at dusk, that should do the trick. He tells me as there are already some o' them braves waitin' in that village. Soon as we swing into action, they'll be

191

in on the game. Others up in the hills'll ride down when they see the flames.'

'Then what? We just spring our mine and take out the sentries?' asked the man on Hilton's right. 'We goin' to look damned foolish if the Indians don't start in at once, once we get goin'. We're like to hang.'

'Ben knows that well enough. It's his neck at hazard, too. If he says those savages are going to war, well, I take him at his word.'

The other man, who had not yet spoken said, 'How much paper money you think there'll be here in the fort?'

Hilton rubbed his chin and said thoughtfully, 'There's the paymaster's office over yonder. I couldn't say how much, but a fair to middlin' sum, I'll be bound. We'll have the pick of what's in the town too, remember. Sundown's in maybe three hours. We best start bringin' in and stowing our supplies here.'

★　★　★

Melanie was standing almost in the very same spot that Talbot had left her, but she was no longer alone. Three young men were surrounding her; not in a menacing way, but simply intrigued to find such a young girl standing around by herself, without a male protector to be seen. When Talbot arrived, they did not at first seem inclined to move on, but continued to banter with Melanie in a way that the older man found a little much. He said, 'Any o' you fellows have sisters? Is this how you'd like to think of men speaking to them? I'd think you'd be ashamed to carry on so.'

Two of the boys went off, looking a little sheepish, but the remaining one said pugnaciously, 'What're you, man, her pa?'

Talbot regarded the youth without saying anything for a second or two, before observing mildly, 'Before you get into a scrape with a man, always be sure it's worthwhile. That how you feel about this present case?'

The young man stared back at him for a moment, before turning and muttering, 'No, I reckon not.' There was something about Talbot Rogers's bearing and general demeanour which, young as he was, caused him to realize that crossing him would not be a wise move.

After the boys left, Talbot said, 'I want you somewhere safe, young Melanie. Not hanging around a street corner in this wise, so that you're in the open when the lightning strikes.'

The girl glanced up to the sky.

'Lightning? You expecting a storm or something?' she said.

'In a manner of speaking. Leastways, I want you tucked out the way, that's all you need know of the matter.'

10

Melanie was less than enchanted with the poky, smelly little room, scarcely bigger than a broom closet, which Talbot Rogers succeeded in securing for her in a log-built house on the far edge of the settlement. She said, after the owner had left, 'Why, it's no better than a pig pen!'

'That's as maybe,' said Talbot shortly, 'but I want your oath that you'll not set foot from here 'til I fetch you.'

She bridled a little, but in the end agreed, as he had known she would. After all, her options were strictly limited and the girl knew that he had her best interests at heart.

Having, as he hoped, secured the safety of the child with whom he had unburdened himself, Talbot left the little house and stood watching the gate of the fort. It was coming on towards evening and the little village was evidently gearing up for some fun. Somewhere, an accordion was playing and there was the cheerful sound of men's voices raised in banter and debate as they got drunk in the nearby saloon.

While he stood there, a glimpse of movement caught Talbot's eye from the huddle of tepees on the other side of the fort. It looked like men moving from one tent to another, but not strolling or sauntering, like they might if they had nothing much on their minds, but swiftly and stealthily. Then he saw another man scuttle from one tepee to another and as he watched, Talbot Rogers was put mightily in mind of soldiers darting from cover to cover as they approached an enemy position. All his lawman's hackles rose as he observed these actions and he knew at once that he was watching something suspicious and probably illegal. It was then that out of the corner of his eye, he caught sight of one of the men he had bumped into at the fort. This man was sauntering along as though he didn't have a care in the world and he was heading towards the gate of Fort Williams.

Something had been nagging away at the back of Talbot's mind ever since he had stumbled into the man and ascertained that he was carrying a concealed weapon. The red bandana had indicated to him that he was probably the self-same man who had galloped past them earlier that day; the one he half-suspected of having shot and killed Melanie's father. Now he suddenly knew what it was he had missed and he cursed himself, thinking that it showed how slow he was getting as he grew older. The fellow was the spit-image of one of those that he and the man from the Indian Bureau had killed during the failed robbery of the stage. It was his brother or some other close kin, for a bet.

Standing there, trying to figure out the best course of action to take, Talbot

Rogers felt the bristly hairs on the back of his neck rise. It was that same feeling that one sometimes has during a thunderstorm, when lightning is about to strike and the air is filled with a sudden electrical tension. All the pieces of the puzzle were coming together in his mind and Talbot knew that the plot, about which the dying man had charged him to carry word to Fort Williams, was about to ripen. The danger in the air was palpable and as he stood there, he saw two more men, Indians he supposed, dart from cover among the tepees and race to a tent on the edge of their village, the nearest to the gate of the fort.

The earth shook and there was a roar like thunder. For the merest fraction of a second, Talbot wondered if lightning had literally struck, but then he saw a column of smoke begin to rise from inside Fort Williams and it was plain to him that some mischief was afoot.

★   ★   ★

Smuggling three quarts of lamp oil and a five pound keg of powder into the fort had been easier than Hilton and his companions could possibly have imagined. The trader who dealt in powder and shot at the ramshackle little settlement in the lee of the fort had been only too cheerful to supply Tom Hilton with five pounds of powder. Acquiring the lamp oil had been similarly straightforward and neither of the men selling these commodities had evinced the least uneasiness in the transactions.

Although the guards at the gates of Fort Williams were very alert to the danger of Indians trying to infiltrate their base, it never for a moment struck them that they would have anything at all to fear from other white folk. The lamp oil was simply shown openly and a wink told the sentry that here was some kind of racket being pulled; maybe somebody selling stolen goods on the cheap to one of the officers or something of that kind. He laughed and waved the man through, seeing nothing

199

that should concern him. Tom Hilton himself took through the powder, as he didn't trust any of his men with this, the most ticklish aspect of the whole business.

Tearing up an old shirt had enabled Hilton to make two long bags from the sleeves. He had tied the end of the sleeves up tightly and then filled them with the gunpowder. In this way, it had been possible to hang them down the inside of his pants, suspended from his belt. It gave Tom Hilton a bit of a spraddle when he walked, but it probably didn't strike anybody that he was carrying enough powder on his person to kill a dozen or more men. At any rate, the sentry just waved him through in a bored and lackadaisical fashion.

From chatting to a couple of the troopers, one of Hilton's men had found that the soldiers ate in the mess hall in three sittings. The first was at six. It now lacked just fifteen minutes to the hour. One of the kegs that the men had brought into the fort was empty and dry; for which reason that the soldier on guard duty had taken no interest in it. Once they were safely inside Fort Williams, Hilton and another man ducked behind a shed and as quickly as they could, hoisted the bags of powder from Hilton's pants and poured the contents into the little wooden barrel. A length of fuse stuffed into the bung-hole completed the preparations and provided them with a compact, but serviceable mine.

There was only one entrance into the mess hall, which was through a narrow porch. This porch was piled with wooden boxes and coils of rope. It was absolutely perfect for what Tom Hilton had in mind. He and the others waited until the first group of men had left the mess hall and the others had gone in to eat. Acting as though they had a perfect right there and were just delivering some goods, Hilton placed his mine on top of the pile of boxes. Around it, the others carefully positioned the kegs of lamp oil. Then, with no more ado, Hilton took out a box of Lucifers and struck one. He held it to the fuse, until it began sputtering and fizzing, whereupon he and the other three men walked briskly away in the direction of the main gate.

The other members of the band were walking from the white settlement towards the Indian village and could be glimpsed through the gate as Hilton and the two others approached the two soldiers who were standing sentry-go there. The 'breed was with the other men, which was important, for without his presence when the uprising began, there was every likelihood of Hilton and other whites simply being massacred along with everybody else.

As soon as they heard the roar of the explosion, Tom Hilton and his companions reached into the back of their pants, pulled out the pistols which were concealed there and shot the two sentries in the back before they had even had a chance to react to the sound of the mine being sprung. Then the three assassins simply walked out of the fort and joined the rest of the gang, walking quickly, but with no sign of undue haste such as might excite attention, to the nearest tent of the Indian village.

The 'breed ushered the other men to a large tent which stood on the very edge of the Indian encampment. It was important that the white men were safely out of the way when the fighting began, because at that point it would be open season on anybody who wasn't obviously Indian. Ben wanted to be sure that anybody could tell at a glance his own origins. Touchy though he sometimes was about not being accepted as a white man, he was at times happy to slip into a different role. The other men noticed that the 'breed was now wearing a headband and hanging prominently around his neck was some necklace of feathers and shells.

When all the members of Hilton's gang were hidden in the tepee, Ben said, 'You boys best not show your faces outside at all, leastways not 'til I give you word. Don't even look out the door, you hear what I tell you?'

'You running this outfit now?' growled Hilton. 'Sounds to me like you're givin' orders.'

The 'breed shrugged and said coolly, 'You want to leave before I get back, then go right ahead. I tell you now, you'll be shot down like dogs. Once the killing's over and folk've calmed down somewhat, we'll take what's due to us and dig up. It's nothing to me if any of you want to go out 'fore then. Your blood'll be upon your own heads.'

Tom Hilton suddenly chuckled and said, 'Ah, don't mind me. Getting scratchy, I guess. We'll sit tight. Be sure and fetch us soon as it's safe.'

*   *   *

As soon as he realized that there had been an explosion inside the fort, Talbot knew immediately that this was the beginning of the rising of which the man from the Indian Bureau had sent warning. For a fraction of a second, he stood undecided, his impulse to run and make sure that Melanie was safe, fighting with his fixed conviction that he should try and save Fort Williams from destruction. The sharp crack of pistol fire made up his mind for him and reminded Talbot Rogers where his duty lay. If Fort Williams fell, then there would be no safety for any white person between here and the Rio Grande.

He moved towards the open gate of the fort. To his left Indians, their faces besmeared with war-paint, were sprinting in the same direction. Their attention was not upon him, though. So insignificant was Talbot in appearance, that he had almost the ability of a chameleon for blending in to the background and not drawing attention to himself. The gate was wide open and as the warriors rushed through, emitting warbling cries and firing their pistols towards a group of soldiers who were running towards a fierce blaze which was engulfing one of the buildings, Talbot slipped through and then moved quickly to one side of the gate. Unless anybody looked directly at him, he was likely to remain unseen.

After taking stock of the situation, Talbot figured that the first task of all was to close the gates and prevent any more young braves swarming in. A brisk fire fight was raging over to one side of the parade ground. For their part the Kiowa, who he assumed these men to be, seemed to be armed mainly with pistols. Some of the cavalry troopers were carrying their carbines, which were being used to deadly effect. As a consequence, the Indians were now sheltering behind buildings and snapping off shots to try and pin down the soldiers and prevent them from making a rush to overwhelm the attackers.

From all that Talbot was able to apprehend, the band of Kiowa who were now inside the compound had not the slightest chance of taking control of or destroying the fort. If he was any judge, the soldiers would soon counter-attack and drive them out. Presumably, other Kiowa were on their way here and these men were no more than an advance party, whose job was to stop the men inside Fort Williams from closing the gates and defending their base against a serious assault. His job then, as he saw it, was to close the gates, so preventing any more Indians from entering the fort.

★　★　★

It was obvious to every one of the men huddled in the tepee that a battle was raging at no great distance from them. Bob Easton said, 'You think Ben's friends are comin' out on top?'

'I couldn't say,' replied Hilton, 'I surely hope so. Else we might as soon've headed south and saved ourselves the trouble of this detour.'

'What if the army wins?'

The other men looked at Tom Hilton, to see what answer he would make to this. He said at once, 'I been giving the matter some thought. If what the 'breed says is right, there's a large body o' men ridin' down on the fort this minute. Still and all, if those horse-soldiers come out ahead, it wouldn't be healthy if they thought we'd had any part of it.'

It was generally accepted that their leader was fond of the sound of his own voice, but this was one of those times when all of the others in that tent were all thinking the self-same thing; that they wished Tom Hilton would just speed it up a mite, stop talking for the sake of it, and get to the point. Maybe Hilton sensed something of this, for he said, 'No matter what the 'breed said, I'm a going to have a look-see out the door and see what's what. 'Cause if the army are getting the upper hand, we need to be with them, not the Indians.' Having said which, he moved to the flap closing off the entrance to the tepee and peered cautiously out. It was plain that what he saw was not to his liking, for he muttered, 'Goddamn!' under his breath and then stood up.

* * *

Casually and not behaving in the least as though it was anything important, Talbot Rogers walked over to the gates of Fort Williams and pushed them closed. All the while, he more than half-expected to feel the sickening thud of a bullet striking him in the back, either from the Indians or perhaps from some trooper who hadn't the wit to make out the play yet. Even as he made his way towards the stout beam of wood which secured the massive gates in place, Talbot smiled to himself wryly at the idea of being killed by one of the soldiers he was aiming to save.

The Kiowa were all about twenty-five yards from the gate now, either lying on the ground or hiding behind buildings as they tried to pin down the soldiers and discourage them from making a determined assault. It was plain to Talbot Rogers what the strategy had been and he felt an unwilling admiration for the band of braves who were prepared to put their lives in danger in this way. He guessed that the main force was even now riding down from the hills. Obviously, if the men on the sentry walks overhead had seen a large body of riders heading towards Fort Williams, they would have closed the gates and sounded the alert. This way, while those men who had infiltrated the Indian village kept the army occupied, there would be no chance of closing the gate. When the attacking force arrived, they would simply ride in and take the fort by sheer weight of numbers. It was a sound enough scheme, but he, Talbot Rogers, was the man to put a spoke in it!

Most of the Indians had their backs to him and were too fully engaged in exchanging shots with the cavalry to notice that behind them a colourless-looking little man was strolling over to the gates of Fort Williams and closing them. All except for one brave, who, noticing what was happening and perhaps divining what was in Talbot's mind, left his fellows and came charging at full speed towards the gates, pulling an enormous dagger from his belt as he did so. It was not one of those occasions where it would have been prudent to try and parlay, so Talbot Rogers simply drew his pistol and shot down the man while he was still half a dozen yards away.

The gates were closed, but it was still needful to raise up a heavy beam of wood and place it through the brackets affixed to the back of the gates. The firing of carbines increased substantially and Talbot guessed that at least some of the troopers had figured out the play now and were intent upon not giving the Indians a chance to look around and see what was afoot. As he stooped down to try and manhandle the bar into place, the crackle of musketry swelled and rose, until it sounded like one continuous, rumbling roar of thunder.

★   ★   ★

Tom Hilton said, 'They've closed up the gates of the fort. Something's gone awry.'

'We best not be found here in a tepee then, I reckon,' said Easton. There were murmurs of agreement.

Tom Hilton had two great strengths which tended towards making him a fine leader of a gang of bandits. One was that he never hesitated for the merest fraction of a second when it came to shooting or any other kind of bloodshed. The other was his ability to change plans without dwelling on the past, agonizing over the course that events had unexpectedly taken or indeed wasting any time in thought at all. The moment that it became clear that the Kiowa had somehow screwed up, Hilton knew that he and his men would have to throw in their hand with the white folk living in the nearby settlement on the other side of Fort Williams. With a little luck, they might even be able to represent themselves as the saviours of the situation.

'Well, what are you bastards waiting for?' growled Hilton. 'Sooner we start helping put down this here rebellion, better it'll be for us. You none o' you recollected that according to the 'breed, there's an army of them savages ridin' down on us this minute?'

The realization that they would not after all be looting the Paymaster's office at the fort was a bitter blow, but there are worse things in this world than not being afforded the opportunity to steal a heap of money. Being hanged as traitors to their race and country was one of those things. If the army had the least suspicion that Hilton and his boys had been mixed up in the uprising, then nothing would save them from summary justice. If the soldiers didn't do for them, then the white folk in the nearby village would. Their best option now was to kill a few Indians and try and avert disaster for the men and women living next to Fort Williams. This was a sound strategy on another level, too. Finding the gates of the fort held against them and the army ready and waiting for them, the Kiowa might not be in precisely the mood to abide by any previous agreements made with some half-breed. They would not likely be inclined to massacre any white men upon whom they were able to lay their hands.

So it was that Tom Hilton and his men emerged from the tent and sprinted towards the white settlement to raise the alarm and alert the citizens there to the fact that at any moment, a vast number of Indians would be riding down on their town to destroy it and kill them all.

11

Melanie heard the explosion at the fort and, like others, thought momentarily that it was a roll of thunder. Young as she was though, glancing out of the window at the cloudless, blue sky told her that this was improbable. Then when the rattle of gunfire began, she knew suddenly that she might once again be caught up in a dangerous situation. The only thought in her head was at once to seek out the only person she trusted to protect and take care of her. Forgetting all that had been most forcibly impressed upon her about the desirability of remaining in the room and not setting foot outside it, the girl slipped through the door and in another minute was standing in the dusty track which served as the main street of the little huddle of buildings which would, one day in the not too distant future, grow into the town of Fort Williams.

There was chaos in the street, with men running hither and thither, shouting and waving weapons about. Nobody appeared to know what was going on, other than that, from the sound of it, a war had broken out. Melanie couldn't see Talbot Rogers anywhere, but then she suddenly heard him. From the sentry-walk of the nearby fort, there was a stentorian bellow. A man yelled at the top of his voice, 'Hey, you people. Attend to what I say!'

The men milling about fell silent and looked up to where Talbot Rogers was cupping his hands around his mouth in order that his words should carry more clearly. When he was sure that he had gained their undivided attention, Talbot called down again, saying, 'There's a large crowd of riders heading down from yonder hills. Indians, by my guess. Get your womenfolk indoors and make ready to defend yourselves.'

Melanie drew breath to shout up to

Talbot, but as she did so, there was a renewed outbreak of furious shooting from the fort and the man on the sentry-walk vanished instantly. The girl's heart leaped into her mouth, with the fear that she was now left alone and with nobody to look after her. There was no chance to brood further on this alarming prospect, as a grizzled-looking old fellow took her arm and said, 'You come along o' me, missy. You can set in our place with m'wife. Can't stay out here, there's like to be gunplay in no time at all.' Melanie allowed herself to be led into a log cabin, which was entered via a door with an exceedingly low lintel.

*   *   *

Lifting up the heavy beam and slotting it through the brackets to secure the gates of the fort against attack was no mean feat for a man of Talbot Rogers's age and physique. Having accomplished the task without being gunned down in the endeavour, he felt a little out of breath but if he was right, there was not a second to lose. Once he was assured that no reinforcements could easily enter Fort Williams to relieve the beleaguered group of Indians who were now pinned down by the army's fire, it was necessary to warn those outside the walls of the fort and let them know the danger that they were in.

Ladders led in several places up to the walkway which encircled the walls of Fort Williams. Talbot made his way up one such and, when he had gained the narrow planks along which sentries and lookouts patrolled, he looked across to the distant hills. A cloud of yellowish-grey dust was being kicked up by what looked to be a body of riders at least 200 strong. If these were Indians and they had arrived just a few minutes earlier, then Fort Williams would have surely fallen. As it was, it was going to be touch and go.

Talbot Rogers cupped his hand round his mouth again and hollered a warning down to the men and women he could see running about like headless chickens in the village below. Then a bullet went droning past his ear and Talbot knew it was time to make himself somewhat less of a target, which he promptly did by the simple expedient of throwing himself flat on the planks which made up the sentry walk, so that he was no longer silhouetted against the sky.

★   ★   ★

Tom Hilton glanced up when he heard somebody shouting from the fort. The firing was more sporadic now which, combined with the circumstance of the gates being closed against intruders, gave Hilton reason to suppose that the army were most probably gaining the advantage. It was a pity, but there it was. He and his boys still had the bearer bonds and there was nothing to hinder them from riding south, as had originally been the plan. Still and all, it would have been a fine thing to be able to loot the fort.

The men living next to Fort Williams were galvanized into action by the warning which Talbot Rogers had shouted down to them. The women were sent indoors and those men who had not been carrying weapons raced to their homes in order to arm themselves. When the half dozen strangers were spotted, approaching from the direction of the cluster of tepees, a couple of the men gave them odd looks. Tom Hilton was ready for this and spoke out at once. He shouted, 'Lord, what ails you folk? Ain't you afeared as you'll be overrun? Let's get those carts across the street here and make this place defensible. Those Kiowa'll be coming from across yonder. You need to prepare!'

As he spoke in this way, Hilton and the men from his band began hauling crates from the front of a little store, as well as manhandling a buggy and a farm wagon so that they partially blocked the little street at one end. So confident and manly did he sound, that the townsfolk who had a few minutes earlier been at a loss to know how to proceed, took their lead from him and began erecting a barricade across the end of the street facing the gates of Fort Williams. In next to no time, Tom Hilton had managed to slip easily into the role of a man of action who knew just what needed to be done and was ready and willing to lend a hand in aid of complete strangers in their hour of need. Once again, Hilton's gang thanked their lucky stars that they had such a versatile and quick-witted man to guide them.

*　　*　　*

Meanwhile, young Melanie was about to make an astonishing discovery. The cabin in which she had been lodged for safekeeping if, as seemed only too likely, there was to be shooting, was cramped, dark and none too fragrant-smelling. The old woman who had been charged with taking care of her had sat Melanie down at a table and offered her a glass of cold buttermilk. As she poured this out from an earthenware pitcher, she said, 'What's your name, honey?'

'Melanie.'

'Well, ain't that a coincidence? I got a granddaughter by the self-same name. Pretty name, sight better than Susan, which is what they call me.'

'Does your granddaughter live nearby?'

'Ain't seen her since she was but six months old. Her pa, which is to say my boy, he had a fallin' out with his wife and he upped and left her and the baby. I've had no dealings with the child or her mother since.'

Outside the little shack, the distant gunfire, along with the shouting and tumult in the street outside, seemed to have subsided somewhat. The old woman gave Melanie a sharp glance and said, 'For why are you lookin' at me like that, miss? What's wrong with you?'

For a moment, the girl did not reply. Then she said, 'I was just wondering if . . . that's to say, if I can ask, what's your son called?'

'That's a strange thing to ask. His name's Clarence. What of it?'

Melanie stood up and said in a choked voice, 'I reckon then as I'm your granddaughter. My father's name was Clarence.'

For all that she seemed so uncompromisingly tough, the old woman looked for a moment as though she might be about to faint with surprise. She said, 'That's my boy, all right. You travel here with him? He here now?'

The enormity of the events of the last few days caught up with the girl and she gulped back tears, before saying, 'He's dead, ma'am. Shot dead some days since. I'm sorry.' Having said which, Melanie burst into tears. The old woman enfolded the child in her arms and also began to sob; the two of them standing there, clinging to each other and weeping. From without came the sound of renewed shooting, mingled with the ululating cries of Indian warriors. Battle had evidently been joined.

* * *

What in later years became known as the Battle of Fort Williams began unfavourably for the men and women in and around the fort. They were vastly outnumbered by the Kiowa forces which had descended from the hills with no other thought than to rid their land of the white men. The advance party who had attempted to seize Fort Williams were all dead now and troopers who joined Talbot Rogers up on the sentry-walk gazed in awe at the huge body of riders that was heading towards them.

'Lord almighty,' observed one young fellow, 'there must be nigh on a thousand of 'em.'

Talbot, whose military experience was a good deal more extensive than the boy who had given this estimate, said, 'I should think more like 400 or 500. But it's likely to be plenty enough for what they purpose. Unless we can pull a rabbit out of the hat, that is to say.'

A sergeant, who had also climbed up

to spy out the strength of the enemy, said, 'You seem acquainted with war, sir. I reckon we owe you thanks for closin' up the gate.'

There were just over a hundred men in Fort Williams who were capable of bearing arms. At least a couple of dozen had been killed by the explosion at the mess hall and there were a fair number of casualties suffering from burns and blast wounds. Little could be done for these men, all efforts being focused upon surviving the onslaught from the Kiowa. Two young officers took command of the fort's defence. Half the men were sent up onto the walkway to lay down intensive fire upon the attackers, while the rest were divided into two parties. If the Indians did finally over-run the fort, then they would pay a heavy price for doing so.

Talbot had his own ideas on the best way to proceed and once it was clear that the sentry-walk would be needed by the men with carbines, he made his way down a ladder and sought out one of the officers. The first he found was Captain Philips, the adjutant with whom he had earlier had an interview. When Philips saw Talbot, he called him over and said, 'I'll allow you were right about our danger. Will you fight along with us now?'

'I will. What of those in that little town? You're going to open the gates and let them in?'

'It's not to be thought of. The Indians'll be upon us in a few minutes. It would take fifteen or twenty minutes to gather up all the folk from those buildings and shepherd them in here. I can't risk having the gates open when the Kiowa arrive.'

★ ★ ★

The Hilton gang were actually enjoying themselves. It was an amusing novelty to find themselves working for once on the side of law and order and they threw themselves into the role with enthusiasm. Tom Hilton had, almost without anybody in the town noticing the fact, more or less assumed command of the defence. He had been the first one to suggest building a barricade and his natural talents as a leader had come to the fore. He was directing men who had been living next to the fort for years in what they should be doing and where they should position themselves. Apart from the pleasure gained through the strange experience of throwing in their lot with the citizens of a little town, there was of course a very good reason for Hilton and the others to oversee the defence of the huddle of buildings. There could be little doubt that any previous deal with the Indians was now off the table and that any white person would most likely be killed in the event of a victory by the Kiowa forces. Tom Hilton and his men were now fighting for their lives just like everybody else.

The first wave of riders which galloped up to Fort Williams presumably expected the gates to be standing wide open, their brethren pinning down the bluecoats inside the fort and hampering any action to oppose the main body of the attackers. As it was, they were no sooner in range of the men on the walls than the firing began. For the troopers up on the sentry-walk, it was at first like a turkey shoot and they set up a withering fire on the Kiowa, causing the main body of them to turn to the right and head round the side of the fort. This led them towards the town and its hastily erected defences.

The flimsy barricade of boxes and barrels, which had been erected at Tom Hilton's urging, was swiftly swept aside and the band of marauders galloped along the main street, firing at windows and men as they rode through. Their aim was not to engage too long with the people living alongside Fort Williams, though. They rather wished to pass straight through the line of wooden buildings and emerge at the other end of the single street, which gave out onto the side wall of the fort. Another group of riders had swerved to the left when they encountered the stiff opposition at the wall overlooking the gates of the fort and were now making their way along the other side, heading towards the rear of Fort Williams.

Three of the Hilton gang were killed in that headlong rush as the Kiowa warriors burst through the barricade and raced towards the rear of the fort. Hilton himself was unscathed and, as usual when the action began, was feeling that heady exhilaration which comes only from escaping death by a narrow margin. It was at times like these that he felt truly alive. He shouted to the men who had been taken aback by the sudden onslaught, 'We must get inside the buildings now! Fire at them from cover.'

Inside the fort, things had taken a turn for the worse. The wooden sentrywalks had only ever been intended to support the weight of one or two men strolling up and down. Once it became apparent that the Indians were sweeping around to the back wall, there was a general rush in that direction. The creosoted wooden tree trunks of which the outer wall of the fort consisted were exceedingly flammable and it was imperative that nobody was given the chance to kindle a fire at the base of the wall, otherwise the whole place was apt to go up like a torch.

It was as two dozen troopers ran from the sentry-walk at the front of the fort, to drive off the riders who were now threatening to encircle the whole fort, that disaster struck. As the soldiers stampeded along the walkways, trying to get to the rear wall, there was a splintering sound and with a screeching of nails being wrenched loose and wood snapping, the walkways on one side of the fort, and also at the rear, collapsed under the unaccustomed weight which they were bearing. Two dozen men were precipitated fifty feet to the ground, many of them breaking arms and legs or fracturing their skulls in the process. In that instant, Fort Williams was deprived of about a quarter of its defenders and the collapse of the sentry-walk on the rear wall of the fort meant that that section was now left completely unguarded.

Captain Philips knew that the situation was critical but that there were still two cards to play. He ordered two men to stand by to open the gates when the order was given and then detailed half a dozen others to make the necessary preparations for what would follow. There was no time to tend to the wounded men who had fallen from the sentry-walks. If the fort fell, then they would all be massacred anyway. Without the ability to direct fire downwards upon the Indians at the foot of the rear wall, there was only one last gamble to be made. Philips knew that as for his other chance, that was quite out of his hands.

Through the cracks between the timber wall at the rear of the fort, flames could now be seen. It hadn't taken long for the Kiowa to figure out that the best way to deal with the cavalry was to smoke them out. One or two incautious men fired at the wall, hoping to deter the attackers, but their musket balls ricocheted off the hardened wood. Nobody was injured, but the captain ordered them all to hold their fire. The time had come for the last desperate gamble, before the fire took hold. Captain Philips ordered the squad to haul the two field guns into position and aim them directly at the gate. When they were in place, he signalled that the gates of the fort should be thrown open.

Some of the Indians had remained in front of the gates and when they saw them being opened wide, they cried out in triumph. Most likely, they thought that the bluecoats were aiming to parlay or even surrender, as there was no sign of any of the cavalry riding out to confront them. The bulk of the warriors, alerted to this new development, surged around to the front of the fort and prepared to ride in through the open gates. There were over 200 of them, bunched up together, as they trotted forward to occupy Fort Williams.

The two twelve-pounder 'Napoleons' had been double charged with canister and as the Kiowa spurred on their horses, convinced that victory was now within their grasp, the captain shouted an order and both field guns discharged their loads at a range of no more than fifty yards. Five hundred lead balls, each considerably larger than a musket ball, ploughed straight into the mass of men and horses. It was sheer carnage and before the echoes had died down, the survivors were being picked off with rifle fire. Without waiting for orders, the men in charge of the guns began reloading them with canister. Then Captain Philips heard the sound for which he had been praying — the clear, metallic note of a bugle in the distance.

Captain Philips was not quite the perfect fool that Talbot Rogers had taken him for. On receipt of the letter warning that the fort was at hazard, Philips had despatched a messenger to the column of troops led by the colonel. Although they had an hour's start, the captain had figured that a swift enough rider might overtake them and pass on the letter from the Indian Bureau's man. So it had evidently proved, because by the time that the second charges of canister had been fired, Colonel Russell's troops had arrived back at the fort and were engaged in fierce combat with the Indians. Faced with such overwhelming force, the Kiowa fled and the threat to Fort Williams was over.

12

It was the day after the battle. Talbot Rogers had discovered, to his great relief, that Melanie was not only safe and well, but that she was now united with her own kin and consequently could be decently abandoned, which was a weight off his mind. There was nothing else to detain him at Fort Williams. He had been profusely thanked by the army and received yet another budget of thanks from her grandmother, and was now, with Melanie and her relatives standing nearby, about to set off in the original direction in which he had been travelling when all this foolishness had erupted.

Talbot had bid his final farewell to the girl whom he had safely delivered from danger and was swinging himself into the saddle, when his eyes fell upon a tough-looking fellow with a bright, scarlet bandana around his neck. This man was strolling past, seemingly without a care in the world.

All prudent considerations urged against pursuing the matter and the wisest course by far was to turn a blind eye and leave others to deal with something which was, when all was said and done, nothing to do with him, but Talbot Rogers was sure in his own mind that this man had had something to do with the death of Melanie's father and quite possibly the attack on the stage. For a moment, he turned the idea over in his mind of doing nothing, but he knew that it wouldn't answer. He could not so easily shake off those years spent in the service of the provost guard. Before he was quite in the saddle, Talbot reversed direction and dismounted again. Smiling reassuringly to Melanie, he walked after the man he suspected of murder and tapped him on the shoulder.

'Yes,' said Tom Hilton brusquely, 'what can I do for you?'

'I think you and me have a crow to pluck, feller,' replied Talbot. 'I mind I seen you once or twice before.'

'Happen so, I get about a bit. What of it?'

Now that he was right up close to the man, Talbot could see that he was indeed the absolute spit-image of the road agent whom he'd shot a few days earlier. He said slowly, 'First off is where I saw you up on some high ground as when this young lady's pa was killed.' He indicated Melanie with a wave of his hand. 'Then again, I've cause to suspicion you for being mixed up in the robbery of a stage.'

Tom Hilton stared at the quietly spoken little man for a space before answering. He noted that although the fellow wasn't wearing a rig, he had a long-barrelled pistol tucked negligently in his belt. He moved back a step, saying as he did so, 'Robbery, hey? Where's your evidence? You the law or what?'

'Evidence? Well, I killed a man who might have been twin to you. Then, some hours later, you show up and shoot dead one o' the men who was on that stage that was robbed. What d'you say to that?'

A subtle change came over the man with whom Talbot was bandying words. He stood up straighter and stared with undisguised detestation and loathing at the man who had called him to account. Tom Hilton, like Talbot, had thought himself home and clear, ready to head south with the remaining men of his band. That was all forgotten now. He had one wish in the world and that was to end the life of the man standing before him, a man who was openly boasting of having killed Hilton's brother.

Unobtrusively and with every appearance of casual indifference, those standing behind Talbot and Tom Hilton moved out of the way. It was not hard to see where this confrontation was heading. Hilton said slowly, 'It was you as killed my brother?'

'If that was the fellow in a bright yellow neckerchief that was molesting an innocent child, then yes. He was part of a gang. 'Less I miss my guess, you're one o' the same outfit.'

'You got that right. You think you can take me?'

'Let's see. Will you come along now to the fort? I aim to hand you over to the provost guard there and they'll arrange for a marshal to come and collect you.'

The calm assurance with which these words were spoken infuriated Tom Hilton to the extent that he could barely breathe; his anger at both that and the fact that his brother's killer stood before him was so great he was almost senseless with rage. Then the man who had taken all this upon himself said in a reasonable and polite tone of voice, 'Well, will you come along with me now?'

There was, according to Hilton's code, no other course of action open to him at this point other than to draw his pistol and kill this mad stranger. Whether Talbot Rogers anticipated this move will never be known. Hilton pulled his gun from its holster and fired twice. Talbot had never been a gunfighter and was certainly not quick on the draw as the other. Howsoever, he had been a soldier and was better able than the average man to take a ball and carry on with what he was doing. As Hilton reached down for his gun, Talbot Rogers knew that he most likely would not be fast enough to fire first, but even so, he made to pluck the long barrelled pistol from his belt.

To those standing nearby, the three shots were so close together that they sounded like a single, prolonged roar. Tom Hilton's first shot took Talbot in the chest, but this didn't hinder his instinctive reaction which was to fire back at Tom Hilton while the other man was cocking his piece to fire again. It was, Talbot noted with satisfaction, a perfectly wonderful shot, which took the outlaw right between his eyes. In his death agony, Hilton let fall the hammer which he had raised with his thumb, sending a ball flying past Talbot's head. Then he fell dead where he stood.

For the briefest moment, Talbot Rogers felt a grim satisfaction in having come out on top in the duel while at the same time exacting justice on behalf of Melanie Barker for the murder of her father. Then he glanced down at his chest and saw that the ball had entered just below his ribs on the left-hand side. He muttered softly, 'Lord, I've been killed.' Then he had the strange impression that the earth beneath his feet was tilting and shifting as though an earthquake was taking place. He lost his balance and crashed into the ground as it rose up to meet him.

For a moment, there was a stunned silence, so rapidly had the drama begun and ended. Then there was a wail of anguish from a young girl standing nearby. She cried out, 'He brought me safe here. He was the best man I ever knew.'

'Come along home,' said the old woman at her side, 'What's done is done.'

. Reluctantly, looking back over her shoulder at the lifeless body of the former lawman the while, Melanie suffered herself to be led away from the scene and back to her grandmother's home. She knew that she would never forget the strange journey which she had made with Talbot Rogers, nor how he had saved her life and avenged her father.